EDGE OF REALITY

D. M. BOURGEOIS

Book Layout © 2023 BookDesignTemplates.com
Book Cover Design by ebooklaunch.com

EDGE OF REALITY/ D.M. BOURGEOIS. -- 1st ed.
ISBN 978-1-7357823-4-8

EDGE OF REALITY

For my sister Deborah:
My sister, my best friend, my guardian angel.
Though death has torn us apart
You will forever be in my heart.

You are still my favorite person.

The bond between sisters is so powerful that even death cannot break it.

—UNKNOWN

CHAPTER ONE

The Mausoleum stood tall with its carved headstones each identifying the entombed remains of the deceased. The buildings loomed out from the dark cover of the massive oak trees that lined the back of the church. Along with the angels perched above her, the stars were mesmerizing and Carsyn was filled with a feeling of serenity and peace. She opened her eyes and looked around noticing the beautiful clusters of yellow wildflowers - she loved the color yellow. A slight slant of her lips was all she could muster before she winced again in pain. She bit down on her lower lip and tried to remain conscious while her mind scrambled to understand what was happening to her. Not knowing where she was or how she got there, she attempted to stay awake.

She felt her pockets in search of her cell phone but came up empty. As she tried to lift her head the ground began to spin. A tear slid down the side of her cheek and made itself at home in the mud puddle she was lying in. Even though she didn't know where she was, her body was aware of her desperate situation.

Carsyn remembered leaving home earlier that afternoon with plans to meet Deacon at The Olive Branch Café for supper. Another round of fierce pain hit, so she held her breath waiting for it to subside. *Something's wrong.* Confused and fighting to control her jumbled thoughts, she focused on locating the origin of pain. She lifted her head again and fought through the dizziness so that she could reach her legs. *There it is. Oh my God!* The Shock of finding a hole in her leg caused her to spin out of control and her vision to become blurry. She leaned her head back down and this time simply gave in to the darkness.

When she woke again, the pain was gone. A quick analysis of her body revealed that something strange was happening leaving Carsyn scared and confused as she gazed at her surroundings. The quiet of the night was so eerie that she welcomed the low sounds of chirping. The instinct to run was overwhelming but her injuries gave her concern on top of not knowing which way to go. There were rows of mausoleums on one side of her, the church on another and then a field that was overgrown with wildflowers. *Yellow wildflowers. I love yellow wildflowers.*

Carsyn's eyes moved over millions and millions of yellow flowers and settled on a beautiful ray of light that was shining in the distance. The brightness was hypnotic and hazy, and she felt herself being pulled in its direction. Her mind was telling her she should be scared but an overwhelming feeling of security took hold, and she knew she was standing in a place of sanctity.

After some time had passed, Carsyn pulled herself up, made her way to the lighted area, and slowly extended her arm so that her fingertips were within inches. Her body trembled with anxiety of what stood behind the haze. She drew her hand back momentarily then thrust it forward right through to the other side of... *What? The other side of what?* Carson was scared, but the feeling of intrigue was stronger. *Veil.* The thin film she was standing in front of reminded her of a veil. The soothing vibes caused her body to slouch as she began to relax and give in to her curiosity. At a closer look, the veil was a beautiful array of tiny floating lights that bounced off one another as if it were swaying to music.

A doorway, she thought, as she continued to examine what had captured her attention. It wasn't large and appeared to be suspended in air. To Carsyn the veil looked to be a temporary doorway, and she wouldn't be surprised if it were to vanish without a moment's notice. She shuddered at that thought and the small quiver deep inside her body brought her back to reality.

Carsyn sensed a change in the atmosphere and reluctantly drew her hand back from the veil. Recognizing that she had been mesmerized and had lost sight of her goal, which was to find a way back to safety, she turned around and canvased the area looking for exits. She was near a heavily wooded area where no one would hear her cries for help. She was all alone, and it didn't take long for fear to creep its way up the back of her spine.

The slight sound of laughter floated through the air and triggered the hair on her arms to stand up and take note. She stood frozen and listened as she tried to identify the sound and the direction from which it had come. Once again, Carsyn heard laughter and what sounded like soft singing.

"When I was just a little girl, I asked my mother what will I be…"

"Hello?" Carsyn barely mumbled the word.

"Will I be pretty, will I be rich, here's what she said to me…"

She swung around and stared into the veil. *Que Sera, Sera.* Carsyn whispered the familiar words.

"Who's there? Can you hear me? I need help, can you help me? Hello?" As fright took hold, Carsyn's legs gave way, and she flopped down to the ground.

The singing, which became louder and louder, grew closer as well. Carsyn pushed herself up again, first to her knees, then back into an upright position. She squeezed her eyes shut and tried to shake off the doomed feeling that was back and clouding her judgement. She listened as the beautiful soft voice continued to sing the song in its entirety. When the singing stopped, Carsyn opened her eyes and gazed into the veil.

"Carsyn." The singing voice now called out to her. "It's me."

"Carsyn come here. Come join me"

Before she had time to react, a hand reached from beyond the veil and pulled her in and away from the only world she knew.

CHAPTER TWO

EARLIER THAT DAY

Carsyn was excited about her new adventure, especially since Deacon was being so supportive. Without him, she would've given into her grief a long time ago. Losing her sister was devastating but with the support of family and friends, she'd learned to live each day without the one person in the world she couldn't live without.

Since that day two years ago, she poured herself into one project after another trying to find something to replace the emptiness that now occupied her broken heart. It wasn't until recently she realized she was running from her grief. Carsyn, with the help of her sister-n-law Avery, concluded that helping people in need was the only thing that made her feel whole again. Avery had no idea what she'd gotten herself into, but she never complained.

The duo's newest adventure was organizing activities at the local Nursing Home. Both women loved scrapbooking and card making. With the help of their friends, Peggy, Linda, and Liz, they had more than enough supplies to make completed projects. Carsyn spent the morning packing up for a class later that day and suddenly realized that she felt peaceful. Her lips curled up and the light shining from her eyes caught Deacon's attention as he entered the kitchen, relieved to see that his wife was smiling again.

"What time is your class today?"

"I'm meeting Avery for 1:30 and the class will start around 2:00." Carsyn was humming in between their conversation.

Deacon stopped his wife as she walked by and pulled her into an embrace.

"It's really good to see you smile. And sing! It's been a long time since I heard that song." He released his wife and headed for the door.

"Where are you off to?"

"Ques Sera, Sera, What will be will be!" Deacon recited the words of her favorite song, the one she was humming, looked back, smiled, then left.

The exchange warmed her heart as she continued packing up for her day. The television was on and before turning it off, she heard the news reporter describe another carjacking in a neighborhood nearby. Carsyn clicked off the remote and headed for the door. She loved the area she lived in, but crime was knocking at the door and that was alarming. *They really need to do something about the increasing crime soon. It's out of control.*

With the car packed and time to spare, Carsyn drove to the local Hobby Lobby to grab more supplies for the day. The sun was bright, but it was surrounded by clouds that were threatening to overtake it and the smell of rain was already in the air. She put the car in park and gathered her cell phone and purse. While exiting her car, she noticed a vehicle parked a few spots over with two men staring at her. A shiver ran up her spine as she tightened her grip on her purse and headed toward the door. *Don't look back. Don't look back.* Against her better judgement, she looked back hoping that she was just overreacting.

Where did they go? Carsyn stopped walking, turned, and looked around the parking lot. The vehicle was still there but she couldn't see the men. *Did they get in that quick?* Nervously, she rushed into the store keeping her eyes wide for any sign of the men. Once inside, she relaxed and headed to the scrapbook supplies aisle. She jumped when her phone rang before realizing she was getting a call. Caller ID revealed that it was Avery.

"Hello." Carsyn answered with a low shaky voice.

"Carsyn? Are you there? Hello?"

She cleared her throat. "I'm here. What's up?"

"Are you okay? You don't sound like yourself. Where are you?"

"I'm at Hobby Lobby picking up the rest of the supplies we need for today's class." Carsyn felt foolish and didn't want to explain why she sounded upset. Distracted by the phone call, she slammed right into a man and jumped back defensively. She rubbed her shoulder where they impacted. *That really hurt!* "Oh, I'm sorry."

"No, excuse me." The man answered and swiftly walked away.

"What was that about? Are you sure you're okay?"

"Yes. Are you there yet? I spoke to Peggy and Liz earlier and they should be getting there soon. Linda had a doctor's appointment and will be there when she can. What time is it anyway?" She focused on her conversation.

"It's 1:30. I just saw them go inside. Are you sure you're alright?" Avery knew Carsyn well and could tell something was wrong by the sound of her voice.

"I'm fine. I'm gonna grab what I need and head that way. I'll see you in a few minutes." Carsyn hung up the phone and subconsciously rubbed her shoulder again as she concentrated on what she needed.

She stayed aware of her surroundings as she strolled through the store. There was a man at the end of the aisle that seemed to be watching her. She stopped and reached for the item on the shelf closest to her basket then turned and went the other way. She took a deep breath and held onto it as she turned the corner only exhaling when she noticed that the next aisle was empty. She glanced down and realized that, in haste, she had put a baby's hat into her basket. Carsyn hated feeling out of control and tried to reason with herself that she was overreacting.

The store wasn't busy, so Carsyn checked out quickly. When she reached the exit doors, she hesitated as the memory of the two suspicious men resurfaced. She inhaled deeply, pushed the doors open and walked out into the parking lot. Relief washed over her as she noticed the vehicle was gone, and the parking lot was almost empty. *Get a grip!* The recent string of car jackings had her on edge and she didn't like feeling that way. There were a few cases reported that involved sexual assault and kidnapping and, in one case, a woman was missing.

She pushed the disturbing thoughts aside, jumped into her car and hit the lock button quickly. *Just in case.* The nursing home was only about 10 minutes away, which gave her plenty of time. The tables were already set up so all they had to do was spread out the supplies for each participant and wait for them to make their way to the room. Most of them were there fifteen minutes early waiting to get started but there were always a few stragglers rolling in a few minutes late. They began the first class with about eight people but each week it grew in popularity.

Carsyn smiled as she thought about the sweet elderly ladies and the way their eyes lit up as the day went on. She could relate, because there was a certain kind of therapy associated with crafting and she always left feeling calm and peaceful. In fact,, Lori, a fellow scrapbooker, held a four-day convention called The Audubon Croppers (TAC), at a local hotel. Over a hundred women attended each year and took pleasure in days of scrapbooking, crafting and most of all relaxing. The 2023 TAC event was coming up the following week. Carsyn and her friends looked forward to it every year.

She was almost at the nursing home and had started to feel excited about the day. She glanced in her review mirror, then put on her signal to turn onto the street leading to her destination. The vehicle behind her caught her attention because it looked similar to the one from the Hobby Lobby parking lot but before she could react, the right blinker started to flash, and the vehicle moved into the next lane. Her shoulders that had unknowingly tensed up, finally relaxed as relief washed over her. She grabbed her phone and quickly took a picture of the license plate before dialing her husband's number. No answer. When she turned the corner, she noticed her sister-n-law in the parking lot waiting for her arrival.

Avery was waiting outside to help Carsyn carry the rest of the supplies in. "You look like you saw a ghost. What's going on Carsyn? And don't tell me nothing because I know you and I know something is bothering you." Avery grabbed hold of her sister-n-law's hand and insisted on getting answers. "Talk to me. What's wrong?"

"I'm alright. When I got to Hobby Lobby two creepy men were staring at me, or so I thought, but when I came out of the store they were gone. I thought I saw the vehicle again behind me on Barataria Blvd., but instead of following me, they moved into the right lane and went straight. I think I'm letting my imagination run away with me. All you hear on the local news are reports of the alarming number of carjackings and kidnappings in and around the city. I know the crime in New Orleans is out of control and has been for years now, but lately the crime has been trickling over to the Westbank of the river and getting dangerously close to us." She squeezed Avery's hand and proceeded to unload the car. "I'm really okay, I promise."

Inside, Peggy and Liz had everything ready and greeted them as they walked in. Seeing her two friends there ready and willing to help tugged at her heart and tears filled her eyes. Linda walked in allowing Carsyn time to turn away and gather herself as she walked up to the front of the class to begin. She had been more emotional lately and didn't want to explain to her family and friends something she didn't even understand herself. While she knew she would never get over losing her sister Cami, she had learned to cope with the loss and with every passing day, was feeling more like her old self again.

The class wrapped up around 3:30 and the five women tidied up the area and chatted about the rest of their day. Carsyn told them that she was meeting Deacon for dinner and wanted to run home and unload her car first. Before leaving, the ladies made plans for lunch the next day and said their goodbyes. Carsyn was the last to leave because she had to stop in the office to schedule the next session. She could've called, but she really liked the event coordinator and looked forward to their short visit.

She chuckled as she thought about the emotional roller coaster she had been on that day. She knew she had been paranoid lately but as she walked to her car, she was feeling confident and strong. Today, she brought a small amount of joy to people who often felt neglected and alone and that made her happy. She started to hum her song again as she walked across the parking lot. She reached for the handle of her car, heard the alarm beep and unlock, and opened the door. Before she knew what was happening, she was shoved to the ground and a large hand covered her nose and mouth with a rag. She reached up to fight back when suddenly everything went dark.

CHAPTER THREE

Everything around her was spinning as Carsyn tried to determine where she was and what had just happened. When she first noticed the veil, it frightened her, but at the same time, she found it inviting. The beautiful site captivated her attention and before long the chaos of the day had disappeared, and a calming peace took over. Now, as she looked back from the other side, the word "doorway" came to mind. *The veil was a doorway, but to where?*

Carsyn stood there admiring the beautiful apparition and the area around her. The sweet chorus of the birds singing surrounded her while the vision of the place soothed her eyes. The Garden of Eden. Carsyn inhaled deeply as she began to absorb the beauty of her surroundings. It felt magical and nothing like anything she'd ever seen. She took a deep breath and twirled around like a little girl. She felt protected and safe. She continued to dance around completely fulfilled and at peace until a hand touched her shoulder and startled her.

"Oh my God! It's you! How? Where am I? How is this happening?" Carsyn's calm peaceful feeling disappeared and was quickly replaced with panic and fear. She wanted to run but every direction looked the same - endless yellow flowers and stunning blue skies.

"This can't be real!" Carsyn covered her face with her hands and began to weep. "This is not real! I know this is not real. I must be hallucinating or bewitched! That's it! The veil! It must have hypnotized me or something." Carsyn's thoughts raced to find answers.

"Calm down! You're being so dramatic as usual. No one has bewitched you although I guess I can see how you might think that, and you're not hallucinating."

Carsyn slowly uncovered her eyes, one finger at a time, and looked up. A shiver ran down her spine as she looked into the familiar face. The shiver was quickly replaced with an overwhelming feeling of love and happiness. She leaped forward and threw her arms around her beautiful sister Cami.

She was afraid to let go worried that Cami would disappear. Maybe I'm dreaming. She tightened her grip and just enjoyed the warmth and love that she felt pour through her body. Her sister's familiar perfume lingered in the air and flooded her mind with wonderful memories of the old days when they had each other to navigate the crazy world. Her lips curled up as she remembered how much they laughed and loved life. They would laugh so hard they would cry and then laugh harder. She missed those days and more importantly she missed her sister.

Reluctantly, she pushed herself back but held on to Cami's hands. She wanted answers but not at the expense of losing her sister again. She increased her hold of Cami's and looked deep into her eyes. She looked just the same as when she left. She was beautiful and radiant, and looked happy. How could she be happy without me? I struggle everyday coping with the loss of her.

"I don't understand what's going on. Oh my God, am I dead? I died didn't I! Oh my God, Oh my God, Oh my God! I can't believe I'm dead! Oh my God! What am I supposed to do? What did you do when you died? Is someone gonna come and tell me what to do?" Carsyn dropped Cami's hands and paced back and forth confused and frantic.

"Would you stop please!" Cami reached for Carsyn trying to calm her.

"Stop! Stop what? Why are you so calm? You should be upset that I'm dead too! How did this happen? I can't be dead. I have stuff to do. I have to meet Deacon for dinner. Oh my God, Deacon. What is he gonna do without me? He's been so patient and supportive since you left, and we were just getting back to normal. I can't leave him yet! I thought we would grow old together. How is he going to go on without me?" She touched her face. "Am I gonna look like this forever? I should've put on makeup this morning. And my clothes." Carsyn's weak voice began to shake. "Why are my clothes torn and full of blood? What happened Cami? Do you know?"

"Yes, Carsyn, I know what happened to you. And no, you are not dead, but you are critically injured and need help soon. I don't know why you ended up here but I'm glad you did." Cami reached out and pulled her little sister in and wrapped her arms around her. "You're gonna be okay. You have to be. I won't let you die. You need to go back through the veil and find help. Your body is lying in the wooded area next to St. Pius X Church. Behind the mausoleum right here in Crown Point. Are you listening to me? Push yourself and get to the road. It's already dark so be careful. Deacon should be looking for you by now. He'll find you! Carsyn, you are so close to home, you can do this. Get to the road and get help."

Carsyn clung to her sister. "No! I don't want to leave you! Cami I'm scared."

"Do you still remember our song, the one mom used to sing to us when we were little? Sing it now. Take a deep breath and sing. I know you can do this!"

Carsyn clung to her sister. "I can't! I'm too scared! I…"

"Yes, you can. You are stronger than you think. Pull yourself together and get ready. You have to hurry. I'll be right here if you need me. I love you Carsyn. Now go!" Cami put both hands on Carsyn and shoved her forward through the veil.

"Stay safe little sister. See you soon! Remember, sing!" Cami did what had to be done.

CHAPTER FOUR

Weak and confused, Carsyn moaned as she moved her body. Aside from feeling pain again, she found herself lying in the same mud puddle as before. She winced as it took hold again. *Was I dreaming? Cami!*

She fought against the pain and sat up. "Cami! Cami! Where are you? Cami, I need you! Don't leave me again! Please!"

Exhausted, she let her body lean back onto the ground. Tears filled her eyes as the first whimper slipped from her lips. I can't do this. I'm too weak. I'm gonna die right here. She wanted to get help, but was physically exhausted. Carsyn's breathing slowed and instead of fighting the feeling of slipping away, she gave in and relaxed as sweet memories of her life came to surface in her mind.

Carsyn began to sing in a whisper. "When I was just a little girl, I asked my mother what will I be. Will I be pretty? Will I be rich?"

Another voice joined in. "Here's what she said to me. Que Sera Sera. Whatever will be will be. The future's not ours to see, Que Sera Sera! What will be will be." Cami urged her sister on. "Carsyn get up! Get up now! You can do it!"

A strong burst of air slapped Carsyn in the face and her eyes flew open. She was momentarily stunned but the sudden surge of energy pushed her to act. She sat up and grimaced. The pain shot through her body, but she refused to let it get the best of her. Move! She rolled over and got onto her knees first. She moved her hands forward, one at a time, and drug her knees behind her.

Her eyes explored the area and noticed a field of yellow wildflowers in the distance. That's St. Pius Church! She attempted to stand up and run toward the church but found her body too weak to comply. She struggled forward dragging her battered body through the rough brush and prickly vines headed toward safety. She was so close to the edge of the woods she could smell freedom, but her body defied her, and she crumpled to the ground again.

"Get up Carsyn! Now! Get up!" Cami's voice vibrated through the air. "You need to push harder. Do not give up! Stop whining and get up!"

"I can't! Everything hurts. Why don't you get help instead of yelling at me? Flag someone down. Go haunt them or whatever it is you do. Please Cami, I'm so tired and weak. I can't move."

Cami stood over Carsyn staring at her. "Are you insane. If I could appear to just anyone, don't you think I would've contacted you by now. I don't know how or why you can see me, but this is all new to me. You watch too many movies Carsyn. Would you have me just walk up to someone and say, 'hey my sister is injured and needs help, so come with me.' What would you do? Run?"

"Maybe you could float up to them instead." Carsyn chuckled soft and low, but Cami knew she was laughing hard deep inside at her ridiculous statement.

"Really Carsyn? That's not funny at all." Cami stifled her own laugh and went on to lecture her little sister. "You are in serious trouble here. You always wanted me to fix things for you but this time little sister you have to get up off your butt and do it yourself. I know it hurts and I know you are tired. You've lost a lot of blood and need to get to the hospital."

Carsyn looked up at Cami and sighed.

"You can see me? You can see me on this side of the Veil? Carsyn, can you see me?"

"Yes, I see you. What do you think I'm looking at, the sky? You are standing right over me yelling."

Cami looked around the area and was fascinated to realize that in her haste to reach her sister, she had crossed over through the Veil to the other side - the side of the living. How was that possible? Before she had time to comprehend the situation, she remembered that her sister was fading fast, and time was running out.

"Get up!" She reached down and tried to pull Carsyn up, but she was unconscious now and her arms slipped right through Cami's grip. "Get up Carsyn! Wake Up!"

Carsyn started to groan, and her body twitched.

"Get up!" Cami screamed so loud that her own body lifted up and was levitating above the ground. "I'm floating! Carsyn look, I'm really floating."

Carsyn opened her eyes and frowned. She watched as Cami floated around in circles and moved up and down swiftly trying to navigate her newfound talent. "Don't all ghosts float? How did you not know that you could do that? Maybe you should've watched more movies with me, then maybe it wouldn't have taken you all this time to realize what you could do. Now really, could you please float away and find me some help?"

"No I can't just fly away. You need to get up. You're almost there. Get up!" Cami reached for Carsyn's arms again and this time she held on for a few minutes longer but eventually they slipped through. "Shoot!"

Carsyn started to cry and reached out for her sister's hand. "Cami, help me please."

Cami sat down next to her and took her hand into her own. "Listen. We need to work together if we're going to get you out of here. This is all new to me. I'm not sure how it all works but I am willing to try anything. Look at me, Carsyn. I need you to concentrate and then grab my hands and hold on tight. I'm going to try and hold on as long as I can and hopefully get you into the opening where someone will see you. Are you ready?"

Both girls closed their eyes and prayed to God for strength.

"On the count of three we are going to do this, okay Carsyn? On the count of three." Cami called "one" and when she reached three, she pulled Carsyn up and the two of them hobbled slowly toward the church.

"We're almost there. Don't stop. You're doing great." They made it past the mausoleum and to the back of the church where Carsyn dropped to the ground and became unconscious again.

"No. No. No. No. No. Carsyn get up. We're almost there." She shook her sister, but she wasn't responding. Cami needed to get help. She ran toward the street and looked in both directions. She didn't know which way to go. Suddenly a car appeared at the stop sign and was turning her way. What do I do? Oh God. Help me. What do I do?

As the car approached, Cami floated out in front of it and let out a horrific scream. The wind drove a sudden gust and the car swerved to the side of the road and stopped. The driver was a young man in his early forties. He jumped out of the car looking startled. Cami didn't know if he could see her. She waved her hand in front of him and yelled "help," but it didn't faze him. He glanced around trying to figure out where the gust of wind came from. He looked toward the church and stared as if something caught his attention.

Cami raced to Carsyn and nudged her to wake up. She was pushing and pulling at her until she finally moved. She groaned each time Cami touched her. Cami hated to do it, but she drew back her leg and kicked Carsyn in the side causing her to cry out in pain.

Cami watched as the man slowly walked toward the church. He stopped and called out. When no one answered, he turned to leave.

"No don't go! Carsyn, wake up! He's leaving! Carsyn!" Cami shook her sister and decided that she had to kick her again.

"Ow! Stop it! That really hurts, Cami!"

"Yell Carsyn! Please yell! There's a man right over there. Yell!" Cami kicked her again.

This time Carsyn screamed so loud the man heard her and ran in her direction.

Cami stood beside her sister and touched the tears that had fallen down her cheek. "It's okay now. You can rest. He heard you. Help is coming Carsyn. Just hold on a little longer. You're gonna be alright. I love you baby sister."

Carsyn opened her eyes and instead of her sister, she saw a man leaning over and calling out to her. She watched as he opened his cell phone and called 911. He placed his jacket over her and assured her that help was on the way. She looked around for her sister but all she saw was a field of yellow flowers and a stranger kind enough to stay with her until help arrived.

Chapter FIVE

S he opened her eyes to total darkness. A thread of panic surfaced as Carsyn tried to assess her situation. She turned her head to the side to get a better hearing advantage. A beeping sound caught her attention first followed by low volume music coming from the small table next to her. She closed her eyes and strained to listen harder. The sound of running water she heard coming from her right trickled to her ears. Someone's in the bathroom.

Her body flexed as anxiety took hold, bracing for another attack. She noticed that she was no longer on the ground but instead laying on something soft. A bed. She was in a bed somewhere inside. As her eyes adjusted to the darkness, Carsyn surveyed her surroundings and finally surmised that she was in a hospital. Her tense body relaxed enough to allow her to put her head back down on the pillow and rest. Her thoughts were all over the place but eventually returned to Cami.

"Cami! Cami!" Carsyn shot up when she remembered her encounter with her sister.

"Cami, where are you?" Screams filled the room.

Deacon watched in horror from the bathroom door as his wife screamed for her dead sister. He raced to her side to comfort her.

"Whoa! Carsyn, honey it's me." He attempted to draw her into an embrace, but she hysterically pushed him away. He put his arms around her and squeezed tight as she continued to cry out for her sister, insisting that she was there. After she had exhausted herself, he loosened his grip and laid her back onto the pillow.

She was pale and possibly still in shock. She reached down to her leg and felt the bandage that had encompassed her entire thigh. The hole she felt earlier was no longer bleeding out. She ran her hand over the sheets that she was lying on and images of the muddy ground surfaced in her mind. I didn't die. As more images flooded her thoughts, she became apprehensive again. I didn't die but I know I was with Cami. Where is she now? She looked around the room for her sister again and prayed that she would be there. Her eyes landed on Deacon.

Her husband smiled at her with hope that she would find comfort in his eyes. He grabbed her hand and slightly squeezed, reassuring her that he was there. She wanted to smile back but she couldn't muster the energy to make it happen. All she could do was squeeze his hand in return before closing her eyes to shut out the world. The hole in her heart was larger than ever and it felt like she had lost her sister all over again. She could not bear it – she won't - not again.

Next time when she awoke there was sunlight shining in the room. Deacon was sleeping on the chair next to her bed. The sunlight that bounced off the top of his head only enhanced his exquisite looks. He was beautiful inside and out. He was not only patient and kind but engaging and supportive. She felt a twinge of guilt as she stared at him and imagined the pain she had caused him when she was fighting not to give up on life. He could've walked away at any time but instead chose to stay and get her through it all. How could she do that to him again? When things were finally getting back to normal, she was going to derail their lives again. She reached out and softly stroked his hand. No, I won't do that to you again. She inhaled deeply and contemplated the fact that she had some difficult choices coming her way.

The door to her room swung open and in walked the nurse. She smiled at Carsyn as she made her way to the hospital bed. She glanced at Deacon and put a finger to her lips.

"Good Morning. My name is Hannah." The nurse whispered as she pointed to Deacon. "He's been here since you arrived. Refused to leave even when he was sure you were going to be alright. How are you feeling?"

"Okay."

"Do you have any pain?" The nurse proceeded to check her vitals while she waited for an answer.

Carsyn shook her head no.

The nurse completed her duties but before she left, patted Carsyn's hand in reassurance that she was there if she needed anything.

"It's going to be alright, sweetie. You just get some rest now."

She was grateful that Deacon was still sleeping. She needed time alone to decipher what was real and what had been a dream. She was certain that she had communicated with Cami. She questioned if that only happened in her mind. She knew it sounded crazy when she claimed her dead sister was there helping her, but she's not crazy. Cami saved her life.

Carsyn retraced the recent events but there was time for which she couldn't account. She remembered meeting Avery, and the girls for their scrapbooking class then the next thing she remembered was waking up in that mud hole. She tried to recall the events between, but they were completely blank. Yellow flowers. She remembered seeing yellow flowers everywhere. The Veil! Carsyn bolted up in the bed. Pain shot through her leg and caused her to cry out. The sound woke Deacon and he quickly got to her bedside to comfort her.

"Good Morning baby. How are you feeling?" He stroked her hair as he stared into her weary eyes. "I'm glad to see you awake. Do you know where you are?"

"The hospital." Carsyn wanted desperately to tell him she was alright to set him at ease, but she couldn't. Tears filled her eyes, but she fought back and refused to cry.

"Oh baby, it's gonna be okay. The doctor said you were going to make a complete recovery. Do you want to talk about it? About what happened to you?"

Carsyn wasn't sure if he was talking about her injuries or seeing her dead sister. Did she tell him that she saw Cami? She couldn't remember what she said to him because everything was a blur. She gave him a slight smile. She needed to hear what he knew because she wanted to protect him from the chaos she was headed for again.

She nodded yes.

"We don't have all the details yet, but the police think that you were car jacked. Do you remember any of that? You were found in the open field behind St. Pius Church in Crown Point. A man said that he was driving by, and a gust of wind caused him to pull over."

Carsyn's eyes opened wide when he spoke those words. Visions of Cami hollering at her to yell out popped into her mind. It was Cami, she stopped that vehicle. It was Cami! I knew it! Her sister was there with her and made sure she survived. Deacon noticed the changed expression in her eyes.

"Baby, do you remember something about that?" Deacon leaned in closer.

She swallowed hard and looked up at her beautiful husband. She wanted to tell him everything but how could she drag him back into the same nightmare they had lived the last couple of years. She had no doubt that he would believe her if she said she saw Cami but that would just be cruel. This was something she was going to have to deal with on her own, at least until she knew more.

She forced a smile again and shook her head no.

Deacon went on to describe the details the man had reported to the police.

"After he pulled over, he got out of the car to find out what had happened. That's when he heard you whimpering. At first, he wasn't sure what he had heard, then you screamed out."

Carsyn chuckled silently. Cami. Her sweet loving dead sister kicked her and caused her to scream out. That proved that she was there. She remembered the excruciating pain she'd felt when Cami kicked her, not once but several times. A slither of hope started to rise up and gave her cause to feel better with each memory that surfaced. She subconsciously rubbed her side.

Her chuckle went unnoticed, and Deacon went on.

"When he found you, he dialed 911 and waited with you until the ambulance arrived. He said you were in and out of consciousness and had lost an alarming amount of blood. The man's name is Ray. He had just moved to Crown Point and was driving by on his way home. The ambulance arrived and brought you here to West Jeff Hospital."

He paused for a moment.

"Does any of this ring a bell?"

She shook her head no, again.

"You were shot Carsyn. You have a small gash on the side of your arm and a gunshot wound to your left leg.

The doctors think that maybe a bullet grazed your arm. The surveillance video from the nursing home confirmed that three armed men approached you from behind and put something over your face. It is presumed to have been chloroform because you went limp quickly and then they shoved you in the back seat and took off. The police are trying to get video from places between the nursing home and St. Pius Church. Did you wake up and try to fight them off? Do you remember anything about the attack?" Deacon was anxious for answers.

Carsyn took a moment before she answered. She didn't remember any part of the attack.

"The only thing I remember is leaving the Nursing home and then waking up in that field. I knew something was wrong, but I had trouble staying awake. I imagine the loss of blood was the cause of that." She stopped there.

She watched as her husband listened to what she said. After she finished, he stared at her waiting for more.

"Is that it? That's all you remember?"

Lord, forgive me. "Yes, that's it." Carsyn felt terrible lying to Deacon but until she could explain how Cami appeared to her, she was going to keep it to herself.

Deacon leaned forward and kissed her forehead before encouraging her to rest. He plopped back down into the chair and turned up the volume on the television. She watched him until he finally closed his eyes. When I know more, you'll be the first one to know my love, I promise. She closed her eyes and within minutes was dreaming of a field blanketed with yellow flowers.

CHAPTER SIX

T he smell of chloroform filled the air and caused her heartbeat to rise rapidly. She opened her eyes frantically. *Where is that coming from?* Carsyn's eyes moved around the room, first stopping on Deacon then moving on. She relaxed again and before long she felt a hand cover her mouth. She flung herself up and out of the bed. She reached for her mouth ready to fight, but there was nothing there. *It must be the medicine they're giving me. Calm down.* She stood silently for a few minutes before deciding that it was safe to lay back down again. She grabbed the remote and turned up the television hoping to be distracted. The local news was on, and it didn't take long to grab her attention. She shrunk down into the bed looking for cover as she watched the news reporter talk about the increase in car jackings in the area and showed pictures of a couple of vehicles the police were interested in.

She shook Deacon and pointed to the screen. "That's the vehicle that was following me. That's it!"

Deacon, still groggy from his short nap, raised the volume as they listened to the report. Apparently, the police captured the vehicle on a video camera in the area of several carjackings, one ending with a missing woman 2 days ago, and a number of simple carjackings since then. The reporter continued the story and ended with a phone number to contact with any information on the vehicle. Deacon grabbed a pen and wrote down the number. He reached in his pocket for the card a detective working Carsyn's case gave him when he took her statement.

He smiled at her before dialing the number. "We're gonna find them. I promise."

She continued to stare at the television screen as the news reporter moved on to other stories. "In other news, government officials are concerned with the accelerated pace AI technology is advancing. There are some concerns…" Her thoughts consumed her, and she couldn't help but think about the poor missing woman.

The image of a hand covering her mouth and the smell of chloroform continued to flood her mind and grew stronger as it went on. She remembered the terror she felt right before it all went black. Carsyn took deep breaths and tried to slow her heart rate down. By the time Deacon finished the call, she was leaning back in the bed and staring at him with big wide eyes. What if they don't catch them? What if they do this to someone else? She pushed the horrifying thoughts to the back of her mind and focused on what Deacon was saying.

"Detective Stevens said they were looking for the vehicle and would keep us updated on the progress. He's going back through the footage from cameras along the route between the nursing home and the church to see if that vehicle shows up." Deacon sat next to his wife and put his arms around her. "I'll keep you safe."

She looked into her husband's eyes and saw desperation and fear. She knew that he was worried just as she was. She hated seeing him like that and wanted to make it all go away.

"Hey. I'm okay. I'm gonna be fine. I won't let them take anymore from us than they already have. The police are going to find them."

The door to the hospital room opened and a tall man in a white lab coat walked in. He was holding a clip board and proceeded to scan over its documents. When he looked up, he smiled and introduced himself to Carsyn.

"I'm Doctor Smith. I'm the doctor that was on staff when they brought you into the emergency room. How are you feeling?"

Carsyn shrugged her shoulders and said, "Okay."

"You were lucky that the wound in your leg wasn't fatal. The bullet missed the femoral artery by a fraction of an inch. You did lose a lot of blood, but I think you'll make a complete recovery. I'd like you to stay here another night just so we can monitor you and then you can go home tomorrow. You'll need to make a follow up appointment with your primary doctor preferably within the week. Do you have any questions for me?"

Again, Carsyn shrugged her shoulder and shook her head no. She didn't want to seem rude, but she couldn't think about anything else other than her attackers. Chills raced up and down her body as the words of the news reporter echoed in her mind. One of the victims is still missing. They could be dead. That could've been me. She wondered how long the victim had been missing. Did they grab someone after they grabbed me? She had so many questions flooding her mind she felt like her head was going to explode. She reached up and covered her ears attempting to slow her thoughts. She still heard the muffled voices of the doctor and Deacon discussing her case. She closed her eyes and decided to try and address each thought that was running rampant as it made its appearance. The attack was the first thought to take shape, so she focused on the details she did remember and hoped that something else would reveal itself along the way. She continued to repeat that process with each thought as it surfaced and froze when she came to Cami. I saw her. She was there. I felt her. I know she saved my life and I need to get back there and find her again. Before she switched to the next thought, she felt a hand touch her arm and she jumped.

"It's just me. Carsyn, honey, it's just me." Deacon sat next to his distraught wife and consoled her. "Did you hear anything the doctor said?"

"I heard everything he said when he was talking to me. I can go home tomorrow. How long do you think that victim has been missing? What if they don't find her? Were all the victims women? We need more information. They need to be stopped before they hurt someone else." Carsyn had decided that she needed to do something.

"Hold on a minute. Slow down. Carsyn, you were shot and left for dead just a few hours ago. You need to focus on your recovery and leave the rest to the police. They will find them and lock them up. Just give them some time to…"

"That missing woman doesn't have much time. What if they dumped her like they did me and she's out there dying alone somewhere? Deacon, we need to do something." Carsyn teared up but wiped her eyes determined to stay strong. She was still frightened, anxious, confused, and angry, along with a whole list of other emotions but allowed anger to take the front seat and focused on finding her attackers and stopping them.

She wondered how much information she could get from Detective Stevens. She needed to find out about the other victims, especially the missing one. She reflected on her own experience and how alone she felt as she lay battered and dying. The chilling fact that she was dumped only a few miles from her home was overwhelming. The area wasn't overly populated but at the same time it wasn't isolated. Carsyn retraced the only two routes that could be used to get to the area where she was dumped. One of the routes leading to the area included many houses along Barataria Blvd. including her own. She was sure that most of those houses had surveillance cameras. The other route that could've been used came off the Highway and turned onto Barataria Blvd. and would've only passed the church. She did know that the church did not have any cameras. She wondered if Detective Stevens had already contacted the people in her neighborhood to look at the cameras.

Carsyn looked over at Deacon and a twinge of guilt rose up in her throat. She didn't want to worry him, but she wasn't going to just sit and wait. He'd been so patient and supportive the past few years and she was grateful, but it was time for her to get it together and stand up for herself. The loss of Cami crippled her for longer than she expected but she was ready to take back control of her emotions and her life.

Once they settled in for the night and Deacon fell asleep, she started to search the internet for similar cases of carjackings in the New Orleans area. The amount of information that popped up was unbelievable and most of it went unsolved. This can't be right! Something has to be done. Carsyn spent the better part of the night reading incident after incident and was sickened by it all. Finally, she put away her phone and decided to get some sleep because when she leaves the hospital tomorrow, she was going to do everything in her power to find her attackers and make sure they were stopped before hurting anyone else.

CHAPTER SEVEN

Carsyn noticed a slight stir of the curtain. Her nostrils flared as the image was registered by her brain followed by the restriction of air to her lungs. She looked around the room and contemplated her next move. By the time she could get out of the hospital bed and run for the door it would be too late. She searched for the help button but noticed that it had fallen to the floor. *A lot of good that does me. I could scream.* Before reacting she went over all her options and determined that they were limited. She glanced at the clock and back toward the window. It was 4:36 in the morning and the hospital was completely quiet. Her attention turned toward the chair Deacon had been sleeping in earlier and it was empty. She did a quick search of the room, but he wasn't there. She reminded herself to breathe as her gaze landed on the curtain again.

"Who's there?" Her voice was so low that she had to strain to hear her own words. Her room was typical of a small hospital room with just the necessities filling the space. The television mounted on the wall had been mut-ed.

Her heart was beating out of control and Carsyn knew she had to make a move. Her best option was to make a break for the door and scream for help. She jumped out of bed and headed for the door, but someone was entering at the same time. She side-stepped and ducked into the bath-room, shutting the door behind her. The smell of chloroform filled the air, and her world was fading fast. The bathroom door opened, she let out a roar, and swung at the empty air. Hands gripped her shoulders and in re-sponse she punched and clawed at her assailant. She continued to scream and fight until she heard Deacon's voice yelling at her.

"Carsyn! Wake up! Carsyn, Honey, you're dreaming! Wake up!" Deacon shook his wife to wake her up. He had awakened earlier and stepped out into the hall to check his phone. He went down to the snack area in the waiting room and when he returned, he heard movement in the room.. He entered, and noticed that someone was in the bathroom.

Confusion crept into her mind as his voice registered with her. Deacon was back and she had to warn him. They were not alone and had to get out of there. She reached up and pulled him close so that she could warn him. He had no idea that someone was in the room with them.

"We have to get out of here. Someone's behind the curtain and we have to go fast." Carsyn was trying to get past him.

"Whoa, honey stop. You're going to hurt yourself. There's no one else here." He helped his wife out of the bathroom and back to bed. He walked to the door and shut it then toward the curtain.

"No! Stop Deacon. They found me We gotta get out of here!"

Deacon pulled the curtain back to reveal to his wife that there was no one there. She watched as he walked back and sat next to her bed. He didn't say a word but instead put his arms around her and waited for her to fall back asleep. She listened as he whispered that it was the pain medicine that was causing her to hallucinate. She knew he was probably thinking the same thing she was, that she was so traumatized from being kidnapped and shot, she would most likely need therapy. Eventually, they fell to sleep.

The door flung open, and the morning nurse pushed into the room. It was only 7:30 and both she and Deacon were still sleeping. She had a rough night and was having trouble recognizing what was real and what was a dream. Watching her husband look at her with concern and worry made things harder. She needed to find out details to find Cami. There was something special about that place and she was anxious to return to get answers.

Carsyn pretended to stay sleeping and was trying to remember what she knew about Irish folklore. The image of the Veil continued to plague her mind and each time she was reminded of the Irish. She tried to recall an old ancient Celtic saying about heaven and earth. Something about places where heaven and earth were especially close. They were called the "Thin Places" from what she could remember. She decided that when she had time alone she would research more of that history.

Her mind bounced back to seeing Cami and how real it felt. Maybe behind the mausoleum in Crown Point was what was referred to as a "Thin" or "Veil" where the two worlds met.

"Ouch!" She opened her eyes and looked at the nurse. She was reminded that she was in the hospital with a serious injury to her leg when the nurse took off the bandage.

"I'm sorry. I know that's uncomfortable, but we have to check the wound and then change the dressing. How are you feeling? Do you need something for pain?" The nurse looked genuinely concerned.

"No. I'm alright. It just hurt a little when you raised it up." She leaned forward to try and see the wound but there was too much stuff in the way. She reached for her side and cried out in pain when she touched it.

The nurse looked up at Carsyn and noticed that she was holding her side. "You have a pretty big area on that side that's bruised. I'm sure it will start to feel better soon."

The memory of being kicked came to mind. *Did they kick me? I don't remember that. But then I don't remember much about the attack.* She explored her memory hoping something would eventually come to her. *Cami! You kicked me! I remember now. You kicked me so that I would scream out for the man. I knew it! I knew you were there! The vision of you was real.* Carsyn smiled and subconsciously rubbed her side again as her thoughts rested on her sister. They were inseparable and would still be that way had fate not intervened. There wasn't a day that passed when she didn't ache from missing her sister. The time passed on, but that emptiness never went away. *Where are you Cami? I still need you. Why aren't you here?* She pocketed those thoughts and focused on the present eager to find out when she was going to be released. She wasn't sure how or why she was able to see her sister or exactly how a "veil" worked. She just knew the clock was ticking and she didn't want time to run out.

A final checkup gave way to her release from the hospital with specific instructions for wound care and a follow up. Carsyn smiled and thanked the doctor. She was excited to be going home to her own bed with Deacon next to her. She watched as he thanked the doctor and asked him a few questions. With no specific plan in mind, she started to devise a few different scenarios that would get her to get back to the cemetery and to Cami. Due to the recent events, Deacon was going to be more overprotective than usual, not letting her out of his sight.

Avery. She'll help me. She's not gonna like it but she'll do it anyway. I can always count on her. Carsyn dialed the phone and waited for her sister n law to pick up. Together they would find the answers she needed and hopefully find Cami.

"Hey it's me. What are you doing later today because I'm gonna need your help." Carsyn listened to the silence from the other end of the phone waiting for Avery to catch up. She knew she was trying to come up with a nice way to say no because that had always been Avery's first response. Of course, they both knew that she was going to help in the end, but they had to go through the motions.

"Carsyn, you really need to go home with your husband and get some rest. Why don't we talk about whatever it is you want me to do in a few days? I know you want to find…"

"Avery, I will get plenty of rest, but I need to do one thing first. Please, I need you and I feel like time is running out. Just come to the house this afternoon and listen to what I have to say. Please." She knew her sister n law and knew she could convince her to help.

After more silence, Avery agreed to hear her out but made no promises to help. That was all that Carsyn needed to hear. They said their goodbyes and disconnected the call. Carsyn let out a sigh of relief, finally able to breathe. She inhaled a deep breath and then slowly exhaled. Since she woke, it was the first time she felt relaxed, and knew it was because she would see her sister again. Soon she would have her answers.

CHAPTER EIGHT

Surprisingly, Carsyn was released from the hospital rather quickly and she and Deacon were relieved to be headed home. She laid back on the headrest and closed her eyes. She didn't want to admit it but getting into the car was difficult and caused her quite a bit of pain, much more than she had expected. The last time she had a pain pill was earlier that morning and it was administered through the IV by the nurse. She hated to take pain medication and had planned to use Tylenol or Advil when she got home. If necessary, she'd take stronger doses, but would avoid the prescribed pain meds all together.

Deacon helped her into the house, and settled on the sofa. She asked him to retrieve her Ibuprofen 800mg prescription so she could get it into her system. She hoped when Avery came over the opportunity to go in search of Cami would present itself and she would be able to move without pain. Otherwise, Avery would never allow her to go anywhere much less let her leave the sofa.

While she waited for the medicine, she googled Celtic Sayings. She scrolled through several sites until she found the one she was thinking of. It read: "Heaven and Earth are only three feet apart, But in Thin Places that distance is even shorter." It didn't have the name of the person that said it, and was only signed as Celtic Saying. That was definitely what she remembered, and those few words were like fire reaching down into her soul. She felt exhilarated and for the first time in a very long time, hopeful.

She went on to read a few other articles about Irish folklore and found most of the sites list that same belief of sacred places that the Irish believe contain "thins" or "veils." *That has to be what I saw. I know it. And I know that Cami is there. I wonder who else is there with her.* Carsyn gasped when that thought crossed her mind. Her hand covered her mouth trying to suppress the sounds. She didn't want Deacon to hear and start asking questions. Avery would be there soon, and she needed him to feel comfortable leaving her alone. She started to feel anxious because she realized that her house was only about a mile from the cemetery where she knew Cami was waiting for her.

As much as she tried to suppress her last thought, it stayed front and center. Not being computer friendly, she tried to find more information on how the "Thins" work, but she could only find that they exist. She wondered if Cami was all alone, and that idea sent shivers up her spine. Carsyn searched her memory for details from their encounter. Cami didn't say anything about being alone or with others. *If mom or dad were there they would've been alongside Cami trying to save my life, right? And she would've mentioned that they were there with her unless she didn't have time.* The slight stir in her stomach suggested that she wasn't sure how she felt about the bizarre idea that her deceased parents along with her sister were right behind that veil minutes away from her. She was still digesting the fact that she actually saw Cami and that her sister helped save her life. Positive that the encounter had been real forced her to question how that could've happened. Would Cami still be there when she finally made her way back or was it a one-time occurrence? Carsyn squirmed in her chair as she confronted each notion only comforted by the fact that she would have her answers soon.

She checked her watch and was surprised that it was already late in the day. Carsyn had been lost in her thoughts but was quickly brought back to reality when she noticed the time. Avery was supposed to come by but hadn't arrived yet. Nervously, she checked her watch again. She snatched her phone up but before she dialed the number, Deacon yelled from the kitchen that dinner was almost ready. She typed a quick message to Avery and then smiled as he walked into the living room.

"It smells wonderful! I don't have much of an appetite, but I'll try to eat some."

Deacon grabbed the TV tray and put it across Carsyn's lap. He knew that she wouldn't want to eat but he made her favorite shrimp pasta and hoped that would entice her. As he walked back toward the kitchen his phone rang.

Carsyn strained over the noise of the television to listen. She only caught bits and pieces but knew that it was someone from the hospital. While she waited for him to return, she checked her messages and saw that Avery apologized and said that she would get there as quickly as she could.

She adjusted her position again and her breathing quickened. It would be dark outside soon enough. Once daylight was gone, they would have to wait until the next day to get answers. Carsyn didn't know if she could make it through the night without knowing if Cami was still there. Her fingers were turning white as she clutched her phone and accepted that tomorrow might have to do.

Deacon walked back into the room with a puzzled look on his face. He had his phone in one hand and had shoved the other into his pants pocket. He stopped in front of her and said that it was the hospital that had called.

"They said that they found my pocketknife in your room and wanted to let me know that they had it at the nurse's desk for me to pick up at my earliest convenience." He pulled his hand out of his pocket and with it his pocketknife. "I told them that it wasn't mine and that it might belong to the person that occupied the room before you. They said they would reach out to them and thanked me for my time."

Carsyn was so caught up in her own thoughts that she just smiled and nodded. Before they could discuss it further, Avery came through the front door. She smiled at them both and then leaned in and hugged Deacon. From behind his shoulder she mouthed 'Sorry' to Carsyn hoping that she wasn't too upset with her. "Brett stopped by with the baby, and I couldn't get away. Wow, something smells good." Avery sat next to Carsyn. "How are you feeling? You look great. Not really but you already know that. How's the pain? Is there anything that I can do?" Avery knew that Carsyn wanted to go to the cemetery today but that wasn't going to happen. Anyway, there was no way Deacon would've let them two out the door. He'd been worried about her since she lost her sister and was sure to be overly protective of her now that she had been attacked. "What are your restrictions? Do you have to stay off of your leg?"

Deacon and Carsyn answered at the same time but with different responses. Deacon said yes and Carsyn responded no and immediately turned to her husband with a scowl on her face.

"The doctor said I could and should walk around carefully of course. I am not staying in bed or on this sofa every day. I will take it easy and not overdo it, but I will not be bedridden." Carsyn knew that Deacon was only concerned but he needed to back up a little and let her decide what was good for her recovery. She hated to argue with him but if she didn't he'd have her living in a bubble and that was not an option. She reached for his hand and guided him to sit next to her. "Look, I know you only want what's best for me, but I got this. I promise I won't do anything that would slow my recovery. I want to heal as quickly as possible, and I think moving around is an important part of the recovery process."

Deacon disagreed. "Avery, would you like to stay and eat with us?" He headed to the kitchen after conceding to Carsyn for now.

"I wish I could. It smells so good." She looked at Carsyn. "I have to go to the store, and I need to run some scrapbooking supplies over to Peggy, but I think I'll do that in the morning."

"What time are you going to Peggy's? I might take a ride with you." She hoped that Avery caught on that she wanted to use that as an excuse to get over to the cemetery. Carsyn was upset that they weren't going that night, but she knew that opportunity had passed, and she'd have to wait until the morning.

Deacon stopped at the kitchen entrance, turned to voice his objection, but thought better of it. She wanted to have a good evening with her husband and was too exhausted to fight. She watched until he continued into the kitchen to fix their plates.

"This is delicious. I didn't think that I'd eat much, but I almost finished my plate. Thanks for cooking my favorite meal. I really appreciate all that you do for me. What are your plans for tomorrow?" She didn't wait for a response. "I think you should go back to work. I'm fine here and Avery will be close by if I need her. Besides, Liz called and said she was going to stop by sometime tomorrow. Did you hear back from the hospital about that knife?" Carsyn swallowed her last bit of drink.

"No. It makes you wonder just how good they clean those rooms. I know they said it was on the floor behind the curtain, so how could they have missed it?"

Carsyn spit out her drink. "What did you say?"

"I said they should clean every…"

She interrupted. "No. Did you say it was on the floor behind the curtain?" The color drained from her face and her eyes were riddled with fright. "Deacon, I told you someone was behind that curtain. Someone was in my room. It had to be my attacker." Her voice shook and the words came faster. "Oh my God! They know who I am. Why didn't I think of that before? They have my information and know where I live." She tried to get up, but Deacon stopped her.

"Carsyn stop. Slow down. We don't know for sure that what you're saying is accurate. Let me call the hospital and ask what they found out from the previous patient, okay? Calm down. Breathe." Deacon tried to calm down and reassure his wife even though he was frightened himself.

She was beating herself up that she hadn't thought about this before. While she was ranting, she suddenly realized that they had her keys too. "Deacon, they have my keys! We can't stay here." After her revelation registered with her husband, she urged him to make the call. She prayed they had found the owner but knew that wouldn't be the case.

CHAPTER NINE

After Deacon spoke to the woman at the hospital and confirmed that the pocketknife didn't belong to the previous patient, he and Carsyn packed a bag and headed to a hotel for the night. She was distraught from the news, so she let Deacon make all the arrangements and pack their stuff. They were both exhausted and didn't get much needed sleep.

Carsyn spent the night going over every detail of her abduction trying to recall anything that would help. At first, the trauma of remembering was overwhelming, and she felt like she was reliving the nightmare. She even smelled the chloroform in the air. Then, the image of the hand covering her mouth made her remember how her heart sank as she realized what was happening. The picture of a cross popped into her mind. At first she ignored it, but the mental representation kept appearing to her each time she rehashed the incident. Eventually she fell asleep and dreamed of the man that kidnapped her. The struggle only lasted a few seconds, but she could see that there was a tattoo on his wrist. It was a tattoo of a cross with the name 'Bella' written on it in script.

At first light, Deacon was on the phone with Detective Stevens filling him in with the latest developments. His voice carried through the room and woke Carsyn from her dream. Her eyes popped open, and she took a moment to become familiar with her surroundings. That had happened more times than she wanted it to lately. First in that field bleeding and left for dead. Next waking up in the hospital and now at the hotel. She hated the way it made her feel scared and vulnerable. She considered herself to be a strong independent woman but lately that belief had been tested. She felt like she was in the middle of a storm and was being thrown around like a rag doll. The more she focused on that, the angrier she got. Suddenly words came into her mind. *You will not continue to feel this way. You are not the kind of woman to let a storm consume you. Pull it together and remember that you are strong. You are strong and you will not be stopped. You are strong and you won't be stopped because you are the storm.* Carsyn repeated those words over and over again until she felt calm and in control. *Be the storm.* She grabbed her crutches from the side of the bed and stood up. She walked over to Deacon just as he hung up the phone. She knew that he was going to hate what she had to say but she refused to let anyone weaken her.

"Why didn't you call me. I would've helped you get up. Are you okay?" He noticed the fire in her eyes and knew that something was up.

"What did Detective Stevens say? Is he going to go to the hospital to get the knife? There's probably DNA on it and maybe we can find the man it belongs to."

"I told him everything and he said he would go by the hospital and confiscate the knife. He suggested that we change the locks on the house today and asked about security cameras. I told him there were cameras at both doors, but I think I'm going to get a few more for around the house." Deacon looked up to see that his wife was deep in thought. Both of her hands were together covering her nose and mouth and she was staring at the floor. "Carsyn, did you hear what I said?"

She snapped her attention back to Deacon but was still pondering something. After a couple of seconds the image she was trying to remember popped up.

"A tattoo of a Cross!" She dropped her hands and repeated, "A tattoo. Deacon one of the men that attacked me had a tattoo on his wrist. It was a cross, and the name Bella was written in script in the middle of it. It was on his right wrist, the one he used to hold the rag over my face." The energy she felt from finally remembering something about her attackers surged through her body. She felt empowered and a sense of satisfaction settled in her mind. *I am strong! I am the storm!* She repeated the words quietly in her mind. She felt her fear slowly break away each time she reminded herself that she was not going to sit back and be a victim.

Deacon grabbed his phone again. "I need to call Detective Stevens back to give him this information." While he dialed the phone he asked her if she remembered anything else. He hadn't told her that the nurse described the knife to him and there was a cross engraved on the handle.

"Yes, only that his hand was dark complected. Tanned maybe but dark complected compared to me. That's all." She sat down on a chair and revisited the memory one more time.

After the call Deacon sat down in the chair next to her. "Detective Stevens said that he would check that information out and see if he could find a match. He promised to get back to us as soon as he had any information. He sounded enthusiastic and said that this information was more than they had from any other case. We need to talk about where we go from here. What do you want to do? We can stay here for a few days or go stay with Nick and Avery."

She thought about the two options and instead suggested that they stay at Deacon's shop. It was adequate enough with three offices, a kitchen, two bathrooms – one with a shower, and close enough to home.

"Deacon let's just go to the shop. We don't know how long this is going to drag on and it could get expensive staying here. Besides, your shop would be comfortable, and it has everything we need."

"Are you sure? That did cross my mind, but I wasn't sure you'd want to stay there. I'll get Nick to help me bring a mattress over and I have that old bed frame stored out in the warehouse." Deacon stopped for a minute and a bleak look came upon his face. "I don't want to leave you alone. Maybe Nick can just get help and bring it to us."

"I'm fine and besides you need to install those cameras and change the locks today, remember. Go. I'll call Avery and have her meet me here. Maybe you should park down by their house and walk through the back in case someone is watching the houses and could follow you here."

"Yeah. That's a good idea. I'll go to Home Depot to get what I need and then head that way. Are you sure you'll be okay?" Deacon put both arms around her and kissed her forehead.

She embraced that moment because as soon as he was gone, she would be ready to head to the church. Avery would object but a little crying would convince her to co-operate. Besides, what were the chances that her attackers would return to the scene of the crime? She considered that statement and the idea that maybe they dumped other victims there crossed her mind. What if that missing woman was there? The investigators searched the area, but Carsyn had crawled out into the open before they found her. Did they check the wooded area or just the sur-roundings where they found her? *What if she's out there all alone and dying?* The thought of that made her cringe so she tucked it away for later. She had to get ready be-cause Avery would be there soon.

She smiled as she thought fondly of Avery and Deacon's brother Nick. His real name was Dominic, but he'd always called his brother Nick or Nicky. She preferred Nick. She was glad that they lived close by and even before losing Cami, she and Deacon were remarkably close with them. Carsyn didn't know what she would've done if she hadn't had Avery there when she lost her sister. Avery was more than her sister n law; she was her sister.

She hobbled back to the bedroom to finish getting ready. She found that using one crutch helped her keep most of her weight off of her injured leg. She could walk on it, but the doctor suggested taking it slow and not overdoing it, so she added the crutch. She kept both crutches on the side of the bed for middle of the night bathroom visits. She didn't want to take a chance of being groggy and falling to the ground or worse opening up the wound. She heard a knock on the door and figured it was Avery. Her phone rang at the same time and caller ID showed Avery.

"Hey. Just wanted to let you know that it's me at the door."

"Good thinking. I'm coming now. Just give me a minute." Carsyn grabbed her crutch and headed to the door. She let Avery in and shut and locked the door behind her.

"Now, are you going to tell me what's going on." Avery waited for whatever bizarre story Carsyn had for her.

"You better sit down for this one." Carsyn went on to explain everything starting from the beginning and watched as the details registered in her sister n laws mind.

"I don't know what to say"

"Just say that you believe me. I know it sounds crazy, but I promise it's all true." She ran her fingers through her hair and shook her head. Just saying aloud all the bizarre events of the last several days made her feel so much better. She hated keeping the information from Deacon, but she knew she had a better chance that Avery would understand and accept the truth. And more importantly, she would help her find her sister again.

Avery sat there staring at Carsyn. She knew that she was always getting into all sorts of crazy situations, but she also knew that Carsyn had never lied to her before. She was the most honest person Avery knew and as peculiar as it sounded, she believed that Carsyn believed everything she was saying. She had to wonder if any of it could be blamed on the loss of blood she had or the trauma alone when she claimed to have seen Cami. Whatever the facts, she would help her find the answers she needed because without a doubt, Carsyn would do the same for Avery.

CHAPTER TEN

The car ride to the church was only a mile from her house, but it was taking forever. She didn't know if it was because of the anticipation of finding Cami or that Avery was driving so slowly they could've walked there faster.

"What are you doing?" She glared at Avery to let her know that she was on to her. "We are doing this." Carsyn continued as her voice started to quiver. "I know it sounds crazy, but I swear I saw Cami. I saw her. I felt her. Avery I need to see her again. There's not a day that goes by that I don't think about her. I have so many memories of us, and I try to revisit them as often as I can." Carsyn looked away when the first tear drop rolled down her cheek. She felt uneasy being that vulnerable. She'd worked hard the last year to suppress her grief and move on but suddenly it was too powerful to shut down. "What if I forget her? What if I forget what she looked like or the sound of her voice? I don't ever want to forget her." The tears were flowing, and her throat had tightened up. She heard the soft whimpering and without looking, she knew that Avery was just as emotional as she was.

Carsyn swiped at her eyes and cleared her throat determined to take control of her emotions. She was intent on finding Cami and didn't want anything to stop them.

"Hey Avery. I'm sorry. I'm just scared she won't be there." She reached over and put her hand on Avery's shoulder. "I really appreciate everything you do for me and all the times you've been there when I needed you most. I don't know if I've told you, but I couldn't live without you either." Carsyn needed to lighten up the conversation. "So pull it together girl! I need you right now. And can we go just a little faster, we don't have all day."

Avery sat silently for a moment then let out a burst of laughter. "Yes ma'am. Let's go find Cami."

Carsyn pretended to move on from their conversation, but she couldn't shake one particular memory. The song that her mother had sung to them when they were little was always their "go to" song. When things were good or bad they would remind each other of the message – What will be will be. She and Cami had a special bond that only became stronger after they lost their mother. When their mother died, Carsyn was only twenty-two, and Cami, thirty-one at the time, stepped up and became not only her best friend but a mother figure too. They laughed at everything all the time. She remembered several occasions that laughter was inappropriate but neither of them could control themselves. That's one of the things she missed the most about her sister, the laughter. She could still hear the sound of her laugh and chuckled at the memory. Some days the pain was almost bearable and others, there were no words for the complete emptiness and loneliness that enveloped her soul.

Carsyn shook her head as she attempted to shake off the unwanted memories. She needed to think. She could see that they were approaching the church and needed to be present minded. She sat up straight and wiped her eyes one last time. When they turned into the parking lot, she felt like the air inside the car had vanished. She looked at Avery who was waiting for instructions.

"I don't know for sure. I remember waking up in that field back there and the veil had appeared way on the other side behind that tomb." She pointed to the mausoleum that was behind the church, all the way to the right, before the wooded area. "It was dark but the light that came from the area was so bright it was almost blinding. I can't really describe what I saw other than to say that it was intense and comforting at the same time. I remember being pulled in that direction and instead of fear, I felt peace. Avery, the warmest feeling took over and I think I even smiled for a second."

They exited the car and walked to the front of the church. Carsyn was terrified and at the same time exhilarated at the idea of seeing Cami again. She was so close and wanted to run toward the area where she last saw her but with her injuries, she couldn't. Her emotions were unsettled, and she wasn't sure how to proceed. Avery walked next to her and laced her arm through hers and squeezed tightly. The sky was overcast preparing for a rainstorm, so timing could place them in a critical situation.

She scanned the area again and when her eyes landed on the woods where she had been dumped and left for dead, she froze. The darkness of the cloudy sky had already claimed that area making it difficult to see but it was tattooed in her mind sure to be with her for the rest of her life. The memory of lying there on the ground scared and alone slammed into her mind like someone running into a brick wall. Her eyes widened as she relived those moments and felt those emotions. Her body trembled and she felt like she needed to throw up.

Avery reached out to Carsyn to steady her. "Are you alright?"

She bent over and inhaled deeply trying to suppress the nausea. In between breaths, she assured Avery that she would be alright. She just needed a minute to compose herself and vanquish the bad memories that had impacted her mind. *I am strong and I will not be stopped! I am strong! I am strong! Can't stop me! I will weather the storm! I am the storm!* After some time had passed, the nausea and bad memories conceded, and she regained control. She stood up and forced an uncertain smile hoping to ease Avery's concerned look.

"I'm sorry. I thought I had come to terms with my attack, but the memories crept up so quickly and caught me completely off guard. I'm good now. We need to hurry because we're getting ready to get caught in a storm. Do you think we should walk back into the woods first and then go toward the place I saw the veil or go straight there? I think we should probably go straight toward the veil since we're limited on time. What do you think we should do?" Carsyn was hopping in a circle as if using crutches were second nature and just as fast as she was talking.

"Whoa. Slow down. Carsyn, please stop for a minute and catch your breath girl." Avery grabbed her arm and pulled her back. "Look at me please. I know you think that you are all good, but these things take time. You went through an extremely traumatic experience, and you don't just get over something like that." She noticed the uncomfortable look on her face and wanted to console her. "Listen, let's look for the veil. I don't think you're ready to go back to the scene of the crime. We'll tackle that later after we find Cami. Ready?"

As bad as Carsyn had been feeling, the love and support that Avery was giving her warmed her heart and prompted a smile. She was blessed to have such a wonderful person rooting for her and always by her side. And the fact that she believed Carsyn about the veil and seeing Cami was encouraging. She was afraid that no one would believe her, and she'd be on her own trying to find her sister. She threw her arms around Avery and squeezed. Water glistened in her eyes as she released from the embrace and started walking.

Silence filled the air as they approached the side of the mausoleum. They were only about ten yards from the back of the building and the realization of finding the veil started to feel real. She leaned onto the crutch, grabbed her shirt and shook it as the heat from anxiety coursed through her body. She reached out and grabbed Avery's hand and together they turned the corner and paused. She scoped out the area not quite sure what to expect. She blinked her eyes trying to get clarity as she registered what she was seeing. There were lots of trees at the far end of the church and a small area that was apparently landscaped weekly. To the side of that was a field of endless yellow flowers.

"It was right over there." Carsyn walked toward the spot where she was sure the veil should've been. She extended her hands out in front of her as she moved forward allowing the crutch to fall to the ground. "I know it was here. It has to be here." Pain shot through her leg as dread bubbled up and escaped her lips as she sighed deeply. Dread quickly turned to urgency, and she started to yell for Cami.

"Cami! Cami! Cami please, where are you? I know you are here. You have to be here." Carsyn dropped to the ground in the exact spot that she last saw the veil and wept for her sister. The stabbing in her heart was as strong as the first time she had lost her sister. She tumbled forward and lost complete control of her emotions. She never thought about what would've happened if she couldn't find Cami. She was so sure that she would be there it hadn't occurred to her that she could be wrong. She continued to cry as she gave into the feeling of defeat.

She felt Avery's hand touch her shoulder offering sympathy. She wiped the mucus running from her nose and rubbed the tears from her eyes. She planted both hands on the ground to help her battered and deflated body up.

"Ouch!" She lifted her right hand expecting to see blood. Something dug into her flesh and caused her pain but there was no blood. She felt around the grassy area and stopped on something sharp. She parted the grass and gasped at what she saw. She picked up the item and turned toward Avery.

"It's a bracelet. Avery, it's my bracelet." The two women stared at the object in her hand.

"It must've fallen off your wrist when you dropped to your knees."

"No. No Avery. I wasn't wearing it. I was wearing it when I was attacked. I didn't realize I had lost it until now. Oh my God, Avery, it was here. It must've fallen off when Cami pulled me through the veil. It was here I knew it!" She was on her feet again with renewed optimism. She grabbed the crutch and walked around the area a little longer, but the light had faded, and the first raindrop landed on her arm. She knew the search was over for that day and or until the weather let up.

Carsyn turned to leave but before she did she whispered, "Cami I know you were here and I'm not giving up. I'll be back tomorrow I promise. Please God help me find her." She made the sign of the cross and headed back toward the car. She twirled the bracelet around her fingers and reflected on the day she gave it to Cami. It was a sign and she wholeheartedly believed in signs. Instead of being upset, Carsyn chose to stay optimistic and was determined that nothing would stop her from finding her sister.

CHAPTER ELEVEN

Rather than go straight back to the hotel, they decided to get something to eat. The rain was heavy, and the winds picked up. Surprisingly, Carsyn was famished and feeling better than she had been lately. She was upset that she'd lost her bracelet and didn't realize it was missing but also thankful that she found it. When Cami was sick Carsyn gave her a St. Benedict Protection Bracelet that her good friend Jane had given her from Medjugorje. After she was gone, Carsyn wore the bracelet. There were days when she forgot to wear it but not often.

The rain continued at a steady pace, but the skies were showing signs of clearing. Sitting under the pavilion in Lafitte waiting for their food from Jan's Cajun Restaurant gave them both a chance to reflect on their morning trip to find Cami. Carsyn toyed with her bracelet relieved to have found it.

"What do we do now?" Avery noticed the disappointment on Carsyn's face and felt sorry for her.

Without looking up she said, "I don't know but I'm not giving up." She held up her arm with the bracelet.

"This proves that the Veil was real and that I did see Cami." She watched Avery's eyes for signs of validation and her heart soared when she got it. *She believes me!* "Thank you for not giving up."

"I can't say that I understand any of this, but I know you and if you say you saw Cami and there was a Veil, I believe you. Besides, it can't be coincidence that you found your bracelet at the exact spot you saw the Veil. I think we need to get back there when the rain lets up and explore the area. I'm just not sure how we're gonna pull that off with Deacon hovering over you like a hawk. How many times has he called or texted you since he left?"

"Actually, I've been sending him text messages so that he wouldn't worry so much. I feel bad keeping this from him, but I think I have to for now."

Avery noticed that she was distracted toward the end of her sentence. "What's wrong? What are you looking at?"

"There's a white van that pulled into the parking lot. It looks just like the one that I saw at Hobby Lobby the day I was carjacked." She pointed at the vehicle. "I'm waiting to see who gets out." The jitters were starting to set in while she waited.

Both women were staring out at the parking lot and hadn't notice their food had arrived. Avery jumped when she realized that Lisa, the woman that worked at Jan's, had brought their food and placed it on the table in front of them.

"Oh my God. I'm sorry Lisa. We didn't notice you walk up. How have you been? How's the family?"

"I'm good. Everyone's good. How about y'all? I heard about what happened to you. Are you okay?" Lisa was concerned.

Carsyn shifted in her chair. That was the first time she'd encountered anyone other than family since the car-jacking. At first she was a little uncomfortable with the idea that everyone knew but relaxed quickly.

"I'm doing okay. Just a little on edge. Do you recognize that old white van in the parking lot?"

Lisa followed Carsyn's gaze, and her eyes landed on the van. "I don't think so. It looks like a work van. We get a lot of new people that are doing construction down here, especially for lunch. Do you know them?"

"No. It just seemed odd that no one got out yet." Just as soon as she said the words, the van slowly moved toward the highway and proceeded to drive away.

"It looks like they changed their mind about eating," Lisa said after she watched them drive away.

Carsyn realized that she was sitting there staring at the parking lot while the others looked at her waiting for her to respond.

"Oh! Yeah I guess so. The fried shrimp looks great. Thanks." Carsyn took a bite of her sandwich and waited for Lisa to leave.

"Did you see that van? I couldn't see in the windows, but don't you think it was odd, Avery? What were they doing here if not to eat?" She grabbed her purse and stated, "I think we should follow them."

"Hold on. By the time we get to the car with your injured leg, they'll be long gone. I tried to get the license plate number, but it was so hard to see. I know it was an old Ford Econoline like the one my dad used to use for work. I think the plate numbers were 327 but not sure about the letters. Possibly DJK but the D could've been an O and the J could've been an I. Like I said it was hard to see from here."

"Man, you are good. I didn't even think about looking at the license plate. I'm sorry that I'm a little crazy lately. I just want the men that assaulted me caught before they hurt someone else. I can't get that missing woman out of my mind. I guess they suspect that she's dead by now but what if she's not and in need of help?" Carsyn shuddered at the thought.

By the time they finished their lunch, Carsyn had forgotten about the white van and had enjoyed laughing with Avery. She felt good getting out of the house and was ready to get back to her regular routine. It was Thursday and that's when she usually went to the bowling alley to line dance. Peggy had invited her months ago, and she'd tried to attend as often as she could. She loved the workout she got from the dancing but also loved socializing with the other women. Ms. Cheryl, the instructor, did a great job of teaching the steps to those who didn't know them and making the class so enjoyable. She wondered if Deacon would agree to let her go tonight just to socialize of course. She didn't need his permission but was sympathetic to his concern for her safety. She'd talk him into going with her because she needed something to distract her mind.

They returned to Avery's car and buckled up. Carsyn thanked her again for everything she did to help. They were discussing ideas for their next scrapbook class and both women seemed at ease when Avery first noticed a white van in her review mirror. She hated to upset Carsyn, but she was starting to worry. Before she could say a word the van tapped the back of her car.

"What was that?" Carsyn turned and saw the van extremely close to the car. She tried to remain calm and instructed Avery to go faster. The van lagged back momentarily but was coming up close behind the car and slammed into the back again. Avery swerved but was able to keep control of the steering wheel. She pressed the gas pedal and the car jerked forward. They were on Leo Kerner Parkway, and it was unusually deserted for that time of the day. They just passed the police station, and it would be a few miles before they reached the nearest gas station. The van attempted to get around them, but Avery cut them off and took another direct hit. The impact sent them toward the woods that lined the highway, so she turned the steering wheel and the car spiraled out of control. She let off the gas and finally came to a complete stop facing the wrong way. Carsyn looked back and watched as the van pulled onto the shoulder and was driving back toward them.

She squirmed around and shouted for Avery to go. "Hurry! Avery hurry, they're coming this way." She continued to watch as the van inched closer to them. "Go! Now! We gotta go."

Avery slammed the gas pedal again and maneuvered the car into the right position putting them face to face with the van that was now only about thirty feet in front of them. Everything seemed to move in slow motion after that. Carsyn squinched her eyes as she tried to see inside the van. The front windshield wasn't tinted like the other windows, but the sun was shining directly into the van making it difficult to see. There were two people in the front, and she would swear they were the two men she saw at Hobby Lobby. Her body shook but not because she was afraid but because she needed to identify them to bring them to justice.

Not thinking, she reached for the door handle determined that she was going to force them out of the van. She pulled the handle but before the door opened, Avery jumped into action and the car started to move. She held her breath bracing for an impact and jerked the car to the left before the van could hit them again. She sped away too scared to look back. The van followed but was unable to catch up with them. As they approached the gas station, Carsyn snapped back to reality and noticed that there were two police cars in the parking lot.

"Avery, look. Pull into the Time Clock gas station, hurry!"

She got into the turning lane and turned without stopping as she crossed the highway. The van sped away and turned a couple of streets away from the station into a neighborhood. Avery pulled next to the police cars and Carsyn got out to explain what had happened. She described the van and gave them the license plate number that Avery had remembered from earlier. She wasn't sure that it was the same van, but it sure looked like it to her.

She noticed that Avery was shaking and understandably scared. After they made a report, they decided to go back to the hotel. She called Deacon to fill him in and he suggested that they meet back at the house instead of the hotel just in case they were being followed. He didn't want Avery to go to her house for the same reason.

"Carsyn that was scary. Do you think it's the same men who attacked you? Why would they come back for you unless maybe they think that you could identify them. You have to be careful." Avery was visibly upset but tried to calm her nerves until the next thought crossed her mind. "They followed us from the church! Oh Carsyn, I bet they followed us from the church and then to Jan's. How else would they know where you were? But how did they know we were going to the church? Did they follow us from the hotel this morning?"

"I know. I was just thinking the same thing. Now I'm gonna have to tell Deacon that we went there. I'm just not ready to tell him everything Avery. He wouldn't understand like you do. Please don't say anything about Cami and the Veil yet. I'm gonna tell him that we went to the church but not everything else. Not until I know more okay?"

Avery hated that she was put in the position to keep this from not only her brother n law but also from her husband. "Don't worry. I'll keep it between us until we know more, and you feel like you are ready. But I do think you're making a mistake. Deacon would understand and be willing to help, you know that. And with this newest turn of events, it might be too dangerous not to tell him. I would hate to think what would've happened had we gone off the road into the ditch or the woods. Do you think they were trying to force us off the road so that they could get to you?" Avery rubbed her arms as the words came out of her mouth. "I have goose bumps just thinking about that."

Carsyn didn't answer because deep down she felt it was exactly what they were trying to do and that terrified her. What scared her even more was the idea that Avery could've become their next victim because of her, and she couldn't live with that on her conscience.

CHAPTER TWELVE

Deacon was waiting for them when they arrived at home. Nick was there too waiting to hear what had happened and decide what they were going to do next. Both women felt confident that they weren't followed after they left the Time Clock. They called Detective Stevens and reported the incident and asked if there were any new developments in her case. He informed them that he was exploring different angles and that things were slow going but were moving. Disappointed, they ended the call and started to discuss what precautions they needed to take to ensure her safety. Carsyn hated that everyone was worried about her but was grateful to have their support.

She wanted to get back to that cemetery but wasn't sure what reason she could come up with that would satisfy Deacon's concerns for her safety. She tried to make eye contact with Avery, but she avoided looking at her. That was probably for the best because she wasn't good at concealing her facial expressions.

"Why would someone revisit the scene of the crime? They had to be after you Carsyn." Deacon's voice shook as he spoke. "Are you positive it was the same men that attacked you?"

"I'm positive. Visibility into the van was low but I knew that it was them. And I guess you are right; they are probably after me. Why else would they come back to the church?" Carsyn's eyes opened wide, and she covered her mouth with both hands. "Oh my God! Do you think they were there to dump another person? What if that's why they were there and when I showed up they thought that I recognized them." The horror she felt was unspeakable. She sat stunned and speechless.

"Did you see them at the church? I thought you said that the first time you noticed them was at the pavilion. Think Carsyn, did you see them at the church?" Deacon turned to Avery and asked, 'Did you see them at the church?"

Avery shook her head no but was too shook up to speak.

Carsyn took some time before agreeing with Avery and confirming that the first time she noticed them was when they pulled into the parking lot. *We have to get back to the church. What if someone needed help?*

"Deacon, we have to go to the church. What if someone's in trouble? Please, call Detective Stevens to meet us there if you want to, but we need to go now."

She watched as her husband battled with his conscience, and his need to keep her safe. She expected him to suggest that they let the Detective check it out but was surprised when he agreed to go.

"I know you won't agree but I wish you would stay here and let me, and Nick go. Will you at least agree to stay in the car until we check the place out? Carsyn, you've been through a lot, and I would never forgive myself if you got hurt." He stood and reached for his keys on the table.

Her heart soared with love and respect for her husband because even though it was the last thing that he wanted to do, he was willing to go to the church and look for a possible victim that needed help. She knew it was a long-shot but what if the van was there because they were dumping someone else? The wooded area was uninhabited and would be a great place to dump something you didn't want found. Most of the time it stayed wet and muddy so it wouldn't be good for the occasional explorer that flocked to the area. She stood and hobbled out the door anxious to get back to the church for more reasons than she'd disclosed.

She watched as Deacon and the others reluctantly followed and a twinge of guilt crept up her spine again. Carsyn shook off the feeling and focused on how she was going to search for the Veil without Deacon becoming more suspicious. He was worried about her safety, but she was confident that the van was long gone and probably wouldn't come back since they now knew she recognized them.

They pulled into the parking lot and stayed inside the vehicle scanning the area. From the car, there was no evidence to suggest that someone was there and needed help.

Deacon opened his door, stepped out and motioned for Nick to do the same.

He held up his hand and stared at Carsyn. "You agreed to stay in the car."

Without another word, he turned and walked toward the mausoleum that sat in front of the wooded area. Her eyes followed him and watched as he squatted down to inspect the mud. Her heart pounded a little faster as she observed his actions. She was too far away to see what he was looking at but determined that it had to be tire tracks or footprints.

"Look Avery, they found something." She looked back and realized that Avery had already observed what she had seen and was watching intently.

"Do you really think that maybe they dumped another person here? That's awful. I can't imagine what you went through. You poor thing." Unable to hide her restlessness, she wrapped her arms around her waist and rocked back and forth. "What should we do? You promised to stay in the car but I'm about to go crazy just sitting her."

"I didn't promise or agree to anything. Don't look at me like that. He asked me to agree and just assumed that I did. I know it's just a technicality but there's no way I'm staying in this car. Besides, I need to see if I can find Cami. I was just waiting for them to go into the woods before I got out of the car."

Avery just stared at her sister n law. "I wondered how you were going to pull this off. I knew you weren't going to stay in the car. Deacon's gonna be so mad at you when he gets back and you're not here. Look, they're headed into the woods now, so if we hurry, maybe we can get back before they notice that we got out." Avery opened her door and mumbled, "The things you get me involved in! Why can't I have a normal sister n law that listens to her husband?"

Once outside the car, Carsyn smiled at Avery and said, "You love me just the way I am, you know it. Now let's go find Cami."

The anticipation she felt was so strong that it reminded her of when she was little and would wait for a jack-in-the-box to pop up at any moment. She crossed her arm through Avery's to help steady her walk. The last thing she needed to do was fall and open the wound on her leg.

She was glad to see that Avery was wide eyed and looking around the area as they walked while she focused on the ground in front of her. As they took each step, her chest rose bigger and bigger. She was finally going to see Cami again. Just a few steps further and they would be in the exact spot.

She released Avery's arm and stood still praying that the Veil would be there. When she saw it the first time, it had caught her attention from where she was laying because it sparkled and glowed. She glared forward searching for any sign but all she saw was grass, trees, and yellow flowers.

"It has to be here. Please Cami. I know you are here." She started to panic. Tears were forming at the thought of failure. She glanced back at Avery, who was clutching her chest, and shook her head. "I know she's here because I can feel her."

Carsyn stretched out her arms and leaned her head back to stare at the sky. She squeezed her eyes shut and slowly turned around in a circle.

"I know you're here. I can feel you. Please Cami I need you. Please."

A cold soft wind blew, and both women caught their breath. The leaves in front of them swirled in the air and seemed to move toward the edge of the woods in the opposite direction that Deacon went.

"Do you hear that? Avery, can you hear it? It's Cami." Carsyn looked toward the dancing leaves and saw Cami at the edge of the woods calling for her to follow her.

"Oh my God! Cami!" Carsyn started to rush forward but after the first step, looked down at her leg and was reminded that she had to go slow. She looked back at Avery and saw the confused expression on her face.

"Carsyn, do you see Cami?"

"Look, she's right there at the edge of the woods. Come on. Hurry." She grabbed Avery's hand and moved toward the vision of her sister.

"I don't see anything. Are you sure you saw her? I felt the wind pick up and watched the leaves rustle, but I don't see Cami." Without hesitation, Avery pushed forward following the lead trusting what Carsyn saw.

Before they reached the edge of the woods, Cami disappeared again.

"No wait! Don't go! Where are you?"

She looked around for her sister but as disappointment took over her body, she felt completely exhausted.

"What's happening? I don't understand." Carsyn stopped and gazed into the woods hoping to spot her sister.

The branches and leaves on the trees started to shake but there was no wind blowing. She perked up and gazed into the woods as she felt sure this was a sign from Cami.

"She's trying to tell me something. We gotta go into the woods. She's leading us somewhere."

They walked slowly on the uneven ground and made their way into the woods. The branches on the trees continued to shake in front of them, leading them deeper and deeper in. The light was distorted, shielded by the large trees and brush. She thought she heard something and stopped abruptly causing Avery to let out a low yelp.

"Do you hear that?" She thought she heard a deep sigh which seemed to be coming from the direction in front of them. She whispered, "Listen."

This time they both stood still and that's when they heard a whimper not far ahead of them. Avery moved quickly past her in that direction. Carsyn started to follow but didn't get far before Avery covered her face and screamed. Panic took over as Carsyn limped onward to see what had startled her sister n law. Her legs gave way and as she fell to the ground she screamed for Deacon.

CHAPTER THIRTEEN

D eacon and Nick were deep in the woods that spanned the land behind the mausoleum. The area was muddy from the recent rain which made it difficult to move easily, much less quickly. He'd called Detective Stevens when they were headed to the cemetery to inform him of their plans to check out Carsyn's suspicions. The detective said that he wasn't far away and that he would meet them there. He hated leaving Carsyn in the car but at least Avery was with her. He chuckled silently because when that thought crossed his mind he wasn't sure if that was actually a good thing. Carsyn had a way of convincing Avery to do whatever it was she wanted to do. She was very persuasive with everyone, especially him. He tucked that thought away to discuss on a later date and tried to focus on the task at hand.

He and Nick had followed footprints throughout the wooded area only to be led in what seemed to be a circle. They entered and went to the left carefully searching every inch of the woods. They reached the Intercoastal Canal and continued across the back of the area. So far, they came across a few areas that looked to have had the mud disturbed, but decided to leave it alone until the detective arrived. They also found a dead bird and a large dead alligator that was quickly decomposing. Deacon covered his nose with his shirt and moved on. The move masked the brunt of the smell, but it still radiated through the fabric and caused him to gag. He wondered how the gator died and made a mental note to mention it to the detective too.

Nick was already several feet in front of Deacon and was hoping to get away from the foul pungent smell as soon as possible. Once they were down wind of the dead alligator they stopped and reviewed where they'd already searched and how much of the area was left. He felt a growing sense of unease that he couldn't see the parking lot from where he was standing. He wanted to finish his search and get back to Carsyn. He couldn't believe that she actually listened and stayed in the car. Even though he couldn't see the parking lot or the road that passed in front of it, he could hear the occasional vehicle pass by. The church bells chimed, and Deacon automatically glanced at his watch. He usually loved the sound of the bells but from his current position in the woods and with everything going on, he couldn't enjoy them.

"Man, I think we did a fairly good search of the area. All we have left is this section that heads to the back of the mausoleum and the overgrown fields around the church. I hate to say it but I'm relieved that we didn't find any bodies. I would hate to think that someone was using our little town as a dumping ground for the dead. It's bad enough they dump their old appliances and furniture out on the old highway. What do you think about those few areas that look freshly disturbed?" Nick stopped to reflect on that unwelcome thought.

"I'm with you. I'm glad we didn't find anyone out here. Nicky, I'm really worried about Carsyn. You know how she gets when she feels that something is wrong, or someone needs help. I wish she would agree to go away for a few days, but I know that'll never happen. I need Detective Stevens to step up his game and find these guys before her already slim patience runs out." Deacon delivered a halfhearted laugh and smiled at his brother. "Thanks for being here, man."

"You don't have to thank me. I'm here if you need me, anytime, you know that."

Deacon thought back to all the times that his brother had his back, and those memories go all the way back to childhood. It was a mutual thing between them and with this situation especially, he was grateful for it. He wondered how he felt about Avery always going along with Carsyn's crazy ideas. If that bothered him, he never showed it and he wasn't the type of man to hold back.

Deacon was well aware of his wife's tenacious attitude before he married her and for the most part, loved that about her. But sometimes, especially when she throws caution to the wind, he wished that she could tone it down some. He realized a long time ago that she would never change, and he had learned to accept it. He was sure there were things about him that bothered her, but she never brought it up. That's what made their marriage work, both were respectful and accepting of each other.

"I think I just heard a car drive up. It's probably the detective. Should we head back to the parking lot or finish our search? We don't have that much more to go." Nick lingered and waited for his orders.

"We can do both because the area that's left will lead us back to the parking lot. We'll just go slow and take our time. I'm sure the detective will call out to us when he comes this way."

Deacon and Nick spread out like they had done before and moved slowly through the remaining wooded area. Like before, it was sloppy and muddy, making it difficult to walk through. The silence should have been comforting and serene but instead was unnerving. They tried to examine the trees and the ground in search of anything unusual or out of the ordinary. The footprints were so abundant and went in different directions that they lost track of them almost from the start. One thing was evident, someone had been in these woods recently. Probably a few different people according to the tracks. He didn't think that there was that much interest in these woods. The Jean Lafitte Nature trail and the Barataria Preserve drew the outdoor enthusiasts to the area because they were only a few miles away but still just an insignificant wooded area such as this. The amount of footprints that were there bothered him and deserved further investigation at a later time.

They were about half the way through the remaining woods when they heard a scream, followed by Carsyn screaming his name. All he could think of was that the van showed back up and Carsyn was in trouble. He and Nick rushed toward the screams which were coming from the same direction they were headed in. His pace quickened and he called out to Carsyn several times before he heard her yell that she was alright. *Why is she not in the car? She agreed to stay there.* His anger grew as he sprinted toward her but when he caught site of her, his love for her took over and all he could do was wrap his arms around her and thank God that she was alright. He would have a serious discussion with her later but for right now he'd never been so happy to see her.

After a few seconds, Nick interrupted. "Deacon, dial 911. Hurry."

"I already called them. Nick, is she still alive?" Avery was standing over her husband.

"Yes, but I can barely find a pulse."

Deacon dropped to the ground where a young female was laying on her side in a contorted way. Her mangled hair covered her face, and she was completely still. At first glance you'd think she was dead, but Nick confirmed that she wasn't, so there was still hope. The sound of sirens pierced through the air announcing that they were getting close.

Deacon lifted Carsyn into his arms and carried her back to the car with Avery in tow. He was met at the edge of the woods by Detective Stevens where he urged him to keep going to find Nick and the injured woman. Before they made it to the car, the ambulance arrived and again he directed them to the site of the emergency. He said a quick prayer for the woman, then made sure that Carsyn was safely in the car and away from this upsetting scene.

Nick joined them and together they all waited for the EMT's to come out of the woods. Detective Stevens appeared first and headed to the car to brief them on the situation. Deacon was worried about Carsyn because she seemed to be unusually speechless. He assumed that she was preoccupied and had a million things running through her mind as he did. All he could think about was the fact that he had listened to Carsyn's suspicions and was quick to respond. They may have saved that girls life.

CHAPTER FOURTEEN

The image of the woman muddy, and covered in blood, was disturbing because it reminded her of the ordeal she'd recently endured. She tried to make a connection but had no idea what she had in common with this woman other than the fact that they were both left alive to die alone in the woods. Carsyn was carjacked and after dumping her, they stole her car which was yet to be found. She'd originally thought that maybe they had shot and dumped her because she could identify them from Hobby Lobby but something else was going on. Her hand raised to her mouth when the horrible thought, that maybe there were others that had been dumped there, hit her mind.

"What if there are others? We need to search these woods. There could be others." Carsyn shouted to Deacon and Detective Stevens.

"Hold on." Deacon urged Carsyn to listen. "Nick and I searched those woods and while there were a few areas of disturbed mud, a dead bird and dead alligator, we didn't find anything else." He looked toward the detective. "I do think it might be worth investigating the areas with loose mud that we stumbled across. We didn't want to disturb anything if it turned out to be some kind of crime scene. Nick can show you what we found and save you some time. Right now I want to get Carsyn and Avery home, well to Avery's house at least, and away from here if that's okay?"

Detective Stevens agreed and promised to stop by to update them before he left the area.

Carsyn started to protest but decided that it was probably best that she go home and regroup. Besides, she needed time to absorb what had happened and come to terms with the fact that Cami disappeared again. Avery said that she didn't see her, but she knew she was there. She led us to that woman. They both noticed the unexplained gust of wind that guided them and were grateful that they had followed their instincts.

She felt tired and defeated because she was sure that when she finally found Cami she would get answers to all her questions. Fear crept up her spine when she admitted to herself that there was a good possibility that she may never see her sister again and that even if she did, she would never truly have her back in her life. *How could I if she's dead and part of another world now?* When she first saw her deceased sister she was so happy, and her only thoughts were how good it would be to find her again. Since Cami's death, she had thought about her all the time and for the first few minutes of everyday her heart felt like it had been split in two and one part was ripped out of her chest. Then, she had to force her mind to focus on memories of the happy times they shared just to push forward and feel somewhat normal the rest of the day. To lose her all over again would be unbearable.

She forced herself to refocus on the current turmoil and smiled at Deacon to hopefully put his mind at ease. He had been so worried about her, and she hated that she had caused him anything but happiness.

"What do we do now?" Carsyn was suddenly full of nervous energy and couldn't sit still. She looked to Deacon for answers even though she knew he didn't have any.

"I don't know. I guess we have to let Detective Stevens do his job honey. I do know it's too dangerous for you to be in this area. I know that's not what you want to hear but please listen to me. Please. We need to lay low for a while." He looked at his wife and hoped she understood the severity of the situation. "Can you do that Carsyn?"

"It's funny you said that because I was hoping that I could go to line dancing tonight at the bowling alley." She held up her hand just as he was about to launch a protest. "Before you say anything just listen to me. I really, really need some sort of distraction right now. I know that I can't participate but it's not all about the dancing. It's such a welcoming and happy environment and I love the people there. It's part of my normal routine and I really need to feel normal right now. That's the only way I'm going to settle down and you know that I'm right. You can come with me. You and Nick can have a few beers and hang out. Please." As she waited for his response another thought popped into her mind.

"Hey Avery, did you make it to Liz's house yet?" She tried to make eye contact with her but once again she avoided looking up. "Weren't you supposed to bring her something."

"Yes, but I called her to tell her I couldn't make it." She finally made eye contact with Carsyn. "I really think I need to stay close to home with Nick right now. I can't even imagine what would've happened if we were forced off the road today. I was really scared."

She watched her sister n law shiver as she said the words. Carsyn felt really guilty about involving her in her own messy situation. She looked around the room at three of the most important people in her life with conflicted emotions. She was so blessed to have them and that made her smile but at the same time she felt sadness and guilt that they could get hurt because of her bringing their involvement into a situation that should be handled by Detectives.

"Hey, we can stay home tonight if that's better for ya'll. I can catch up on the new *Love Is Blind* episodes. It's crazy to see Elizabeth and her son Paul on the show."

"How did the watch party go? Didn't you, Charisse, and Thom go to her house and wait until 2am for the show to drop here on Netflix? I saw the pictures you posted. I don't know where you get your energy. There is no way I could stay up until 2am." Avery just shook her head.

Carsyn laughed. "We stayed up all night. The first of five episodes dropped at 2am and we stayed up until 7am and watched them all. It was fun. And surprisingly, I wasn't that tired the rest of the day. The most exciting part was watching how social media reacted to both Elizabeth and Paul. Everyone loved them."

"That's great. I imagine it's weird watching your son get engaged to a woman he just met, but I believe that love can happen quickly. Now, I'm anxious to see what happens next for Paul." Avery was relieved to move on from the idea of going line dancing.

"I think that's a great idea Carsyn. I know you want things to get back to normal but it's gonna take some time. At least give it a few days to see what the detective can find out. Obviously, these men are dangerous, and we don't know if that woman we found today has any connection. I hope she's gonna be okay." Deacon ran his fingers through his hair as the vison of the woman crossed his mind. "I hate to think what would've happened to her had we not listened to you. Carsyn, I know I always tease you about things but I'm glad you pushed us to search those woods today. You may have saved that woman's life."

The images of the body spread across her mind again but this time she pushed it back. She was praying that the woman would be okay but focusing on her was too painful. The reminder of her own ordeal was keeping her anxious and afraid and she was trying desperately to be done with that. And besides the more important task at hand was to find Cami. She looked at Deacon, who was staring at her, and contemplated telling him about seeing her deceased sister. *Would he understand? Would he believe me? He would, but do I want to go there yet?* Her thoughts were all over the place and she needed a quick distraction.

"Hey, what about dinner?" Carsyn's stomach rumbled as she spoke.

"Avery jumped up to offer a suggestion. "Why don't we stay here and order pizza. Not delivery considering everything that's going on and we don't know who to trust but take out. Nick can go pick it up." She looked at Carsyn. "We can pick a Netflix series, one that we can all enjoy, and try to relax. What do ya'll think?"

"I'm in. Just tell me where to go for the pizza." Nick grabbed his keys and waited for instructions from his wife.

Carsyn waited as they discussed the pizza order, called it in, and then settled in for the night. She and Avery searched Netflix for something couple-friendly to watch and after scrolling through the menu, decided to play a game instead. She knew that they had all had enough drama for one day.

CHAPTER FIFTEEN

After a late night at Avery and Nick's house she returned to the shop at around 3am, her new home for a while, and was ready for bed. Carsyn was glad to see that Deacon and Nick were able to get the mattress there and the bed was all set up and ready. She noticed that they had brought her television and had it set up as well. She was too tired to connect to the Wi-Fi so she would be without television for the night.

After she'd showered, she laid in bed and said a few prayers. She said a special prayer for the woman they had found and hoped that she was the missing woman from the news story she'd heard about a few days earlier. Her thoughts were scrambled and jumped from one thing to the other. She prayed that she would find Cami and when she was finished with her prayers she grabbed her phone.

Deacon was showering so she had a few moments to search the internet. She typed in "Irish Folklore" and scrolled down the list that popped up. She read a few articles, but they all pretty much said the same things she'd already learned. *Wait! Father Terry is from Ireland. I can ask him what he knows about the subject. I'll just have to tell Deacon about Cami because I need help.* Feeling optimistic, she made a mental note to call Father Terry in the morning and set up lunch.

Carsyn closed her eyes and was surprised when the picture of the tattoo that was on the arm of her assailant was front and center in her mind. The cross was typical but something about the name Bella was bothering her. She squeezed her eyes tighter and expected the image to become clearer. The name Bella was written in fancy script but there were a few letters that followed. She tossed versions of Bella over and over in her mind hoping to trigger something. The first letter was an "R" and it looked to flow into an "a" or an "o" possibly. She let out a sigh of frustration and was interrupted by Deacon as he sat down on the bed next to her.

He watched as she opened her eyes and stared at him. "How's it going? You sounded a little upset."

She smiled at him. She wanted to tell him about Cami, but she didn't want to worry him. Maybe she could wait until the morning that way he could have a good night's sleep instead of worrying about yet another one of her problems.

"I'm good. I just realized that there was more to that tattoo, but my mind just can't recall the image."

Deacon looked at his phone and noticed that he'd missed a call from Detective Stevens earlier. "Give it some time. You'll remember all the details and then we'll get these guys."

An alert sounded from Carsyn's phone. She checked the notification, and a chill ran up her spine.

"That's the back door Ring camera at home. She opened the notification and gasped. "There's someone at the back door. Deacon look." They watched as a person wearing a hooded sweatshirt attempted to turn the knob of the back door.

Deacon hit the button to speak and yelled, "Hello! Who's there? What do you want?"

She watched as the man looked dead into the camera and glared while he shook the handle again.

"Deacon it's him. Look at his wrist. Bella Rae. It says Bella Rae. Why didn't he run? What are we gonna do?"

She reached for Deacon's phone and dialed 911 and watched as the intruder punched through the back door glass and thankfully set off the alarm system.

"Hey! Get out of here! The police are on the way!" Deacon tried to scare him off again yelling over the loud alarm.

"Oh my God, Deacon, he thinks we're there. He doesn't know that you're talking to him from... Hello, this is Carsyn Trahan. Someone is breaking into my house. I'm not home but I can see them on the ring camera." Carsyn gave the 911 operator her address and then hung up.

She and Deacon sat there helpless as they watched the scene unfold right before their eyes. Once he got the door open, he retrieved a gun from the back of his pants and entered the house. She thought about calling Nick but after she saw the gun was glad that she hadn't. She heard the sounds of police sirens and that caused him to pause. Carsyn wrapped her arms around herself in an attempt to feel safe. She was sick to her stomach because his presence at her home confirmed that he was looking for her and the sight of the gun suggested that he wanted her dead. He turned to leave but the first of the police cars had arrived and were headed his way. He moved straight toward the officer and started shooting as he ran away. Thank God the officer wasn't hit but he had to run for cover himself and that allowed the suspect to get away. The whole scene unfolded within a matter of seconds, and after he was gone, Carsyn sat there too stunned to move. *He wants me dead.* She leaned against Deacon and started to cry.

Deacon put his arm around her but was already on the phone with Detective Stevens. She took a deep breath and tried to gain control of her emotions. She didn't want to make things worse or harder on her husband besides, she was stronger than that. She reminded herself that she was in control and that she would not allow anyone to take away her peace. *I'm not afraid of the storm, I am the storm!* She got up and started to get dressed.

"Whoa, hold on Carsyn. What are you doing?" Before she could answer he continued. "You are not going there. It's way too dangerous. You saw this guy, he's either too stupid or just doesn't care about getting caught. I thought everyone knew about ring voice technology. Maybe he's not from here. But that doesn't matter. You cannot go anywhere near the house."

She saw the terror in Deacon's eyes and although she was ready to face her attackers head on, her heart overruled her drive for justice, and she sat back down to listen. She owed him that much after he spent the last several years listening to her as she worked through the grief of losing Cami. *Cami. I need you Cami, now more than ever. I'm trying to be strong, but the truth is I'm scared. I'm lost. I need you.* She looked up to see relief in her husband's eyes.

The commotion at the house finally settled down and Deacon set down Carsyn's phone. She didn't reply but simply sat there in silence. She turned her head slightly toward the front door because she thought she heard a noise. Her eyes met Deacon's and she knew that he heard it too. He placed his finger over his lips signaling her to be quiet and grabbed her hand. She grabbed her phone and purse and together they quietly rushed to the door that led into the warehouse. Just as she was typing a message to Detective Stevens, she heard glass break on the entrance door. Someone was entering the building. The alarm raged which meant that the police would be dispatched. Deacon rushed her toward the back and into a small room. He shut the door and locked it. She reached into her purse, pulled out her gun and handed it to her husband. Reality was setting in that her assailants were not going to stop looking for her and she wouldn't be safe until one of them was dead.

Deacon took the gun and squeezed her hand. "It's gonna be okay. The police will be here soon. This door is reinforced steel so they shouldn't be able to get in. Don't worry."

Carsyn sat down in the corner of the room and stared at her phone that no longer had service. She knew she should be afraid of the men that were after her, and she was, but what scared her the most was the thought that she wouldn't be able to get back to St. Pius Church to find Cami and time could be running out. She had no idea how things like this worked, was there a time limit on the time Cami could communicate, how long was that time limit, and a ton of other information that would be extremely helpful, but hoped that she could talk to Father Terry tomorrow and get some answers.

"Hey Deacon. I need to tell you something."

CHAPTER SIXTEEN

The absence of noise had her on edge. The room she and Deacon were in was not soundproof but after they locked themselves in, the outside world went silent. Even the alarm that was raging outside the building was muffled in the back of the warehouse and almost nonexistent in the room. While it seemed like they were in there forever, it had only been a couple of minutes.

Just as she was about to confide in Deacon about Cami, the first bullet hit the door. She jumped up and with Deacon shielding her with his body, they both moved to the furthest corner of the room. The bullets continued to riddle the door generating a high pitched sound that caused her to put both hands over her ears. She closed her eyes and held her breath until the noise stopped.

"They're reloading." Deacon looked around the room for safety.

"Oh my God! What are we going to do? Do you think they can get in?" That last question made her shiver.

Her phone lit up and caught her attention. She opened the phone and saw a message from Detective Stevens. "Almost there. Are ya'll alright?"

She read the message aloud and immediately started to reply. She informed him of their whereabouts and that someone was trying to shoot their way into the room. Normally she was a wiz at text messaging, but her hands were shaking so much that she was having difficulty getting it done. Finally she pressed send.

The shooting resumed and she watched as deacon listened intently and appeared to be counting. He was counting the shots. Again the shooting stopped.

"That was fifteen shots. They must be reloading again."

Carsyn jumped when the sound of the shooting started again but this time the bullets weren't hitting the door.

"They're here! The cops are here!" She looked down at her phone again and noticed the one word message – "HERE!"

The sound of exchanged gunfire went on for a few minutes then everything went silent again. She lightened her grip on Deacon's arm but didn't let go. She'd never seen her husband in a situation like this one before and marveled at the way he protected her. He shielded her with his body and was willing to die for her. When she retreated and covered her ears, he was counting the shots and looking for a safer place to be.

The love and support she felt from her husband gave her the strength to calm down and regroup. She thanked

God that they were in Jefferson Parish and that the police response was quick. She'd heard horror stories from around the country of slow to no response when it came to police departments but both Gretna and Jefferson Parish police departments were on top of their game. She couldn't imagine waiting for help that never arrived.

"It's quiet now. I wonder if they left." Deacon was approaching the door.

He grabbed the doorknob and started to turn it when someone banged on the door causing them to jump. Again, her phone lit up telling her that she had a message, so she read it aloud. "All is safe. You can come out now."

Deacon looked at her for approval before he opened the door. She knew that, like her, he was anxious to see what was happening on the other side of the door. She was weary about opening the door but nodded yes. They couldn't stay in there forever. He finally pushed the door open and was greeted by several officers and Detective Stevens. Carsyn was finding it difficult to move toward the door afraid of what was out there. *Did he get away? Was it only one person or were there more? Is he dead?* She continued to watch Deacon and from his startled reaction when he looked to the right she got her answer. Someone was dead. She said a quick prayer that the officers were not hurt.

"Are ya'll okay? Where's Mrs. Trahan?" Detective Stevens rushed past Deacon into the room.

"I'm fine. I just need a minute." Carsyn sat back down and tried to decompress. Watching the man break into her house was hard enough but to be held up in a room that someone was trying to get into to hurt her was over the top. She inhaled and exhaled slowly and started to whisper her song.

"When I was just a little girl, I asked my mother what will I be…"

Before she could finish the first line, a vision of Cami appeared and was standing in front of the door. Carsyn rubbed her eyes and looked up again. The vision was still there.

"Cami! Is that really you? Are you really here?" She pushed herself up from the ground but didn't move forward. She was afraid that if she did, Cami would disappear.

"Yes It's me. Who else would it be? I don't know how much time I have but I wanted to warn you. Those men are dangerous and won't stop until they find you. You need to find a safe place to stay for now." Cami had a grim look on her face.

"I came back to look for you with Avery. I couldn't find the veil, but I saw you guide me to that woman. Did the same men that hurt me dump that woman there? Are there other victims there? How can I find you if I need you? I have so many questions." Carsyn reached out to her sister.

"I told you I don't know. You have access to the internet, do some research."

"Sure, in between the attacks and all the other stuff going on in my life the last few days I'll research 'why am I seeing my dead sister.' I did try to find information on Veils or Thins but there was little on that subject. And you know I'm not the best at research." Carsyn was frustrated.

"Well I'm still learning what I can and can't do. What I do know is you are in danger, and I won't let anything happen to you. And baby sister, be careful who you put your trust in."

Detective Stevens called Carsyn's name, and she looked his way. He was walking toward her asking questions. When she looked back for Cami she was gone. Again her heart shattered at the loss of her sister. *Why does this keep happening?* The pain and agony she felt must've been written all over her face because he ran to her just before she collapsed. He carried her out of the room and past a body sprawled out on a bed of red. She buried her face in his chest hoping to unsee the image. She wasn't normally squeamish but seeing both the woman in the woods earlier and the body on the floor of the shop in one day was more than she wanted to see in a lifetime.

She was carried all the way to one of the offices where she was placed down in a chair. She said thank you and assured him that she was alright. The office door stayed open, and the view of the entire warehouse was available from there. There was a body on the floor, but several officers were blocking her view. Deacon was talking to the Detective who was informing him on the chain of events. Carsyn needed to know what was going on so instead of staying put in the office, she hobbled out to join the two men. The Tylenol was wearing off and the pain was coming to the surface. She glanced down to make sure there wasn't any bleeding through her bandage. Deacon saw her approaching and met her halfway.

"What's going on? Is he dead? Did they catch the guy that was at the house?" Detective Stevens was walking toward her as well, so she directed the last question to him. "Did you find out the identity of the woman in the woods yet?"

"Yes, we know her identity. She's still unconscious but we were able to match her to a missing report filed the day before. Her family was contacted and are with her now." Detective Stevens watched as her hope faded away. "Sorry Mrs. Trahan but that's not the missing woman that you saw reported on the news the other day. Unfortunately, she's still missing."

They continued to talk while the investigators did their jobs examining the evidence surrounding the break in and the body. While they were still discussing the missing women, the coroner's office finished and was moving the body out of the shop. When they passed by, Carsyn gasped.

"Look at his wrist. That's the same cross tattoo as the guy that attacked me. The only difference is my attacker had a name under the cross. Do you think it's some sort of gang tattoo?"

"We're already checking with the FBI because they have a tattoo recognition database. We're just waiting to hear back from them and as soon as we do I'll let you know. My guess would be yes that this guy and the one at your house are in this together and probably part of some sort of gang. But let's not get ahead of ourselves. Right now we need to discuss where you go from here. Apparently, they know a lot about you and that makes things complicated. Is there anything else that you remember about these guys that would explain why they want to get to you so badly?"

"I told you everything I know."

"Think about the surroundings of the Hobby Lobby parking lot when you first noticed these guys. They were standing by a white van. What else were they doing? Do you remember any other suspicious vehicles around? They must think that you either know something or have something they want. We're also doing a face recognition search on the man from your house. He looked directly at your ring doorbell camera, so we have a good picture of him. But that's why I don't think they are after you just because you can identify them. This man didn't care who saw him and I doubt he'll show up in any of our databases."

Carsyn rubbed her forehead with both hands trying to relieve the stress of everything. She squeezed her eyes shut and tried to remember the incident at Hobby Lobby. She visualized getting out of her car and involuntarily shivered as the memory of first seeing the men surfaced.

"I can't recall anything out of the ordinary in the parking lot and to be honest, they didn't do anything peculiar,

I just had a feeling about them. I guess we should always trust our gut." Carsyn looked at the detective with a slight smile. "After I entered the store I got what I needed then I left. They were gone when I came out of the store."

"Did you speak to anyone in the store?" Detective Stevens desperately wanted to find a connection. Originally he thought her attackers might have been part of a sex trafficking ring that was rampant in New Orleans and unfortunately all over the world, but they wouldn't keep coming for her.

"Only the cashier. She was a young girl and I've seen her there many times before. I don't think she could be involved. Do you?" Carsyn was second guessing everything.

"I'm not ruling out anybody or anything. Do you know her name?"

"Tina, I think. Yes, it's Tina. She's early twenties, maybe my height, thin with light brown hair. Like I said, I go there a lot and she's been there for a while." She glared at Deacon because she knew he was about to comment about her frequent stops at Hobby Lobby.

"I'll get someone to check her out. In the meantime we have to decide where you are going to stay until we can find this guy." He glanced out the door as the body was being loaded into the medical examiner's vehicle and was relieved that now there was one less person to worry about. "Let's hope it's just the two of them."

Carsyn shuddered at the thought of the possibility that there were other men after her. It was bad enough to be worried about the original two men. She leaned on Deacon for support while she tried to figure out where she could go to be safe but at the same time, search for her sister. Deacon won't like it, but she won't give up on finding Cami no matter how many people are after her. Nothing was going to stand in her way.

CHAPTER SEVENTEEN

Carsyn and Deacon remained in the office while Detective Stevens finished outside. She was trying to decide on a good place to stay but kept coming up empty. She knew Deacon was struggling too because neither one of them wanted to put anyone else in danger. They were already worried about Avery and Nick since they'd all been together the last few days.

"Why don't we go to the coast for a while. Maybe a week or so just until we get a plan. I'm sure Avery and Nick will come too that way we won't have to worry about them. I know their safety has crossed your mind just like mine." Deacon saw in his wife's eyes that they were not going to be going to the coast.

"I need to tell you something. Before you say anything, let me finish. Please don't interrupt. I don't even know where to begin. I saw Cami! Yes, Cami my deceased sister." She waited for him to say something but instead he just sat there. "When I was lying in the woods bleeding out, I saw a light and what appeared to be a curtain. Deacon it was so bright and beautiful. At first I thought that I had died but soon found out that was not the case. I didn't know what was going on and I was scared but something about the light was soothing. I did some research since then and found out that there is an old Irish folklore about certain places in the world that were sacred and in those places, there was a thin Veil between our world and the afterworld. Sometimes it was referred to as the Thins."

"Why didn't you say something about this before now?"

"I don't know. I was scared I guess. At first I didn't know what to think about it and I wasn't sure if it was real. I had lost a lot of blood and was in and out of consciousness. But Deacon, I've seen her several times since then." A single tear rolled down her cheek.

He wiped a tear from her face and his heart ached for her. He wanted to believe her, and part of him did, but it was all so bizarre. "How do you know that it's real?"

"She saved my life. There's so much to tell you but most importantly, she's here to help me. Neither one of us understands why this is happening but it is happening. That's why Avery and I went back to the cemetery. I was…"

"Wait, Avery knows about this?"

Carsyn reluctantly answered. "Yes. I'm sorry I kept it from you, but I knew you wouldn't want me anywhere near the Church and I had to find Cami. Avery didn't want to help me, but she did, and I swore her to secrecy. I was going to tell you, but I didn't know how and now I'm running out of time." The tears were flowing freely as she pleaded her case.

"Listen, when I couldn't get help and was too weak to call out, Cami kicked me in my side to make me scream. I know how that sounds but before that she floated in front of the man's car and screamed to make him stop. Remember he said all of a sudden there was a gust of wind that took his car? That was her. That was Cami. If he hadn't stopped I'd be dead Deacon. I know it sounds crazy but the bruises on my side confirmed that it happened. Look, they're still there." Carsyn let out a nervous laugh. "I think she got a little carried away, but she saved my life."

Deacon looked at the bruising on her side. He reached out and pulled her into an embrace. "I hate that you had to go through that whole ordeal."

She pushed herself back and looked into his eyes. "I know it all sounds crazy. I do. But when you and Nick were in the woods, Avery and I got out of the car to look for the Veil and Cami. My sister guided us to that woman in the woods. I didn't find the veil and was headed back to the car when a gust of wind passed, and I saw Cami standing in front of the wooded area."

"Did Avery see her? Did she see Cami?"

"No, but the sudden gust of wind convinced her enough to go with me into the woods and that's how we found that woman. Look, there's so much more to tell you but we need to decide where to go before the detective leaves. What are your thoughts, besides leaving town? I can't leave Cami. I won't."

"Nick's rental house is vacant until the first of the month. That gives us a few weeks to lay low there and it's close to home. I'll give him a call to confirm. Go tell Detective Stevens to come back in the office when he's finished." Deacon dialed Nick's number and waited for him to answer.

A weight had been lifted from her shoulders and she began to feel stronger. Knowing that Deacon didn't completely freak out gave her hope that he would believe her. She wondered if the circumstances were reversed would she believe him." She mumbled under her breath "yes" then set out to get the detective.

Carsyn walked outside where the area was blanketed with officers and other first responders. She spotted Detective Stevens and walked over to speak to him. He was standing near the body and had slipped something into his pocket. He turned just as she approached.

"Just wanted to get a good look at the body. We searched him for identification but the only thing he had was a money clip and a cell phone. The cell phone is locked but appears to be a burner phone anyway." He started to walk back into the building as he spoke.

She followed him inside and was updating him on their tentative plans. She heard Deacon talking to Nick and waited for the answer. A sudden feeling of fatigue came over her and all she wanted to do was get some rest. She was tired of explaining Cami and she was tired of worrying about her assailants. She needed some down time and by the looks of Deacon, so did he.

Detective Stevens suggested that they use a few of the first responders uniforms to leave the building. He'd told them that he'd already made the arrangements with a couple of EMT's that were on the scene. They agreed to the switch and would get them safely away from there. As she was putting on the uniform, she couldn't help thinking how crazy everything seemed. Was she really dressing up as an EMT and sneaking out of the building? The severity of the situation began to set in and all she could do was concentrate and go along with the plan.

Both she and Deacon were dressed like first responders, walked out the shop door and got into the back of the EMT vehicle. The rest of the officers and first responders were still out there. There was one man standing at the back that looked suspicious to her, but he turned and made his way to another vehicle. Detective Stevens locked and shut the shop door. He tipped his hat at the driver of the vehicle they were in giving him the go ahead to leave the scene. The plan was to take them to West Jefferson hospital and from there they would be picked up by Nick and Avery. The hospital was only about 10 minutes from the shop so there wasn't much time before the next phase of the plan was to happen.

Nick and Avery were there waiting for them when they arrived. They made the exchange in the parking garage since it was late and there was not a lot of traffic. She wondered about the two first responders that were kind enough to trade places with them and how they were going to get back to their vehicle. The thought of their willingness to help them warmed her heart.

She leaned back against the head rest and closed her eyes. She revisited the events from earlier and smiled as she thought of Cami. The smile quickly turned into a frown when she remembered the last thing Cami said to her. *Be careful who you put your trust in. What did she mean? Does she know something?* As hard as it was to do, she pushed those thoughts out of her mind and tried to relax. She felt a hand cup hers and opened her eyes to see Avery smiling at her. She squeezed her sister n laws hand and before long, went to sleep.

CHAPTER EIGHTEEN

The 15 minute ride to their new temporary home gave her the chance to relax and breathe. The last few days were unimaginable, and she didn't think she could handle any more chaos. But she knew that as long as tattoo man was still out there and after her there would be no peace. She must've been exhausted because she woke when Avery shook her and she had saliva all over her chin. They had arrived at the rental house and both Deacon and Nick were unloading the car. Apparently, Nick and Avery stocked up on everything they would need before they picked them up. Carsyn smiled at them lovingly, feeling blessed to have them in her life.

The rental house was nice, but she couldn't help wishing for her own home and her own bed. She was so thankful that the rental house was an option because she didn't want to be far from Cami, wherever that may be. She didn't even know if she'd even see her again. The thought of that sent a surge of panic raging through her body. Suddenly she felt the air leave her lungs and the world seemed to spin out of control. *No! No! No! I can't lose you again. I know you're out there and I'm gonna find you.* She clasped her hands together and dropped to her knees. *Please God, don't take her away from me again. Please don't!* Deacon ran to her side and helped her up from the floor. She looked up at him with that same expression she had right after Cami passed away.

She was devastated then and was starting to feel the same way again. She was just beginning to accept that she'd lost her sister and was learning to live without her. Avery was a huge part of her recovery and although no one could ever replace Cami, her love helped ease the pain Carsyn endured. She loved her like a sister and the fact that she was mixed up in all this chaos made Carsyn cringe. She couldn't help but to wonder if she'd made a mistake telling her about Cami. If they hadn't gone back to find the veil, she wouldn't be involved. *Lord Carsyn, get a grip!* She hated how out of control she was feeling and needed to rein in her thoughts and emotions.

They settled inside and tried to shake off the remnants of an awful morning. The idea that someone attempted to break into their house and another person succeeded in breaking into the shop was holding on to her thoughts refusing to be discarded. She was getting good at sharing her mind with unwanted thoughts that shook her to her core then putting up a front that suggested she was strong and in control. She just wasn't sure how long she could continue putting up that strong front.

They spent the rest of the day watching television and trying to decompress. Eventually, she and Deacon took their showers and made their way to one of the bedrooms. She was pleased to find out that Avery and Nick were staying with them. They said that they felt like it would be a risk to go back to their house. Someone could be there waiting to harm them or waiting to follow them back to her. Usually, if the four of them were together, they would stay up late chatting, but everyone agreed that it was best to get a good night's rest and regroup in the morning. She knew that it was going to be difficult to fall asleep since it was only 7pm but agreed that rest was needed.

Surprisingly, Carsyn woke up and noticed the sun was shining through the window. Deacon was still asleep, so she tiptoed to the bathroom not wanting to disturb him. She grabbed her phone to check the time. *I can't believe I slept all night.* She must've been exhausted from the stress and running on adrenaline the last couple of days.

Quietly, she went into the kitchen to start the coffee pot. The pot was already full of fresh hot coffee and Avery was sitting at the kitchen table enjoying her first cup.

"Good morning," she whispered.

"Good morning to you. Why are you up so early? Did you sleep any?" Carsyn was worried about her.

"Believe it or not, I slept great. I just got up a few minutes ago. How did you sleep?"

"I slept great as well. We might have to rent this house because I never sleep all night anymore." She smiled as she walked over to the table to join Avery.

"I told Deacon about Cami. He didn't say much but I think he believed me. I don't know what I did to deserve him, but I thank God for him every day." She set her cup down to cool. "That goes for you too, Avery. I hope you know how much you mean to me. Wouldn't want to go through this crazy life without you."

"So what now? Did ya'll talk about how to go forward from here. I hate to say it, but they may never find this guy. I know you don't want to hear that but unfortunately that's reality. Ya'll are welcome to stay here for as long as you need to. I think that we are going to stay a few days and then decide what to do." Avery noticed that Carsyn wasn't listening but instead was preoccupied with her own deep thoughts.

"Carsyn, honey did you hear anything I said?"

She slowly looked up at Avery. "Yes. I heard everything you said, and I know you are right. But to be honest, finding Cami is all I can think about. What if I'm too late? What if I can't find her again? I know how dangerous it is for me to go anywhere near the church right now, but I have to find her. That's my plans. When Deacon wakes up, I want him to go with me to look for Cami. We can walk there for all I care but I am going back there one way or another." She looked away trying to keep her composure.

Avery saw the fire in Carsyn's eyes and knew better than to try and reason with her. "Hey. Look at me please. We are here for you too. If you and Deacon are going back then so are we. Even though I didn't see Cami with my own eyes, I know you did. If I were you, I would do the same thing. Take a breath and settle down for a few minutes. Let's enjoy our coffee and as soon as the men are up I promise I'll be by your side insisting that we go find Cami."

She rubbed her eyes and let her hands rest on both sides of her cheeks. "This is all so... I don't even know what to call it. Bizarre. Crazy. Unbelievable. You know me. I love all those supernatural movies and series but I never in a million years believed that any of it was true. But Cami is here, and she saved my life. I was supposed to call Fr. Terry about Irish Folklore, but, well you know I been kinda busy." She smiled and then before long both of them were laughing hysterically.

All she could think of was "what are we laughing at' because there was nothing funny about the situation, but it felt good to let go. Avery motioned for her to keep it down but that just caused them both to explode into deeper laughter. Before long Avery grabbed between her legs and darted to the bathroom. Carsyn continued to laugh as she recalled that Avery could never get through their spells without running to the bathroom. Her laughter slowly subsided, and she stared out the back door. A beautiful yellow butterfly was fluttering around a mass of yellow wildflowers in the back yard. For a moment, she felt warm and cozy as she enjoyed the site and quietly mumbled, "I love yellow flowers."

"I know you love yellow flowers." Deacon walked into the kitchen and when his words made her jump, he was sorry he'd disturbed her.

She held her hands over her heart and took a moment to recover from being startled. Deacon walked over to her and placed his hands on her shoulders. His touch comforted her, and she relaxed.

"I didn't mean to scare you. Sorry. How did you sleep?"

Before she answered, Avery walked back into the kitchen followed by Nick. She noticed that Avery had on a different pair of shorts which meant that she didn't make it to the bathroom in time. When their eyes met, they almost burst into laughter again but instead she waved a hand and stood up trying to suppress the feeling.

"Good morning Nick. Looks like the gangs all here. Does anyone want breakfast?" She doesn't usually eat breakfast but thought she'd ask. They all shook their heads no, but went for coffee.

"When is your follow up with the doctor for your leg?" Avery was reminded when she noticed the bandage on Carsyn's leg.

"Not until next week and she really should be taking it easy until then." Deacon shot her a look as he answered the question meant for her.

"I'm fine. I am surprised how well it's healing." She pointed at Deacon. "You saw it last night when I cleaned and re-bandaged it after my shower. I know you're worried about it, but I am trying to be careful. With that being said, I have something to say."

"Come on Carsyn. Can we just have a few moments to relax." Deacon had a feeling what was coming.

"Sure you can. But I have to go find Cami."

Nick through up his hands. "Wait, what?"

Carsyn rubbed her eyes again and sighed. "I know, Nick. That sounded crazy. Believe me I know. However, brother-in-law, you heard correctly. I saw my dead sister the day I was attacked. In fact she helped save me. I've seen her several times since then but never long enough to get answers to how that is even possible. But it obviously is and now I have to find her before it's too late."

Nick just stood there dumbfounded and then said, "Alright then. What do we need to do?"

"Whoa wait a minute. We are not going to do anything without first thinking this through. We need to remember that someone is out there looking for you Carsyn and we need to be careful." Deacon was voicing his opinion even though he knew there was no way he was going to stop her from going after Cami. "Can we at least come up with a plan first?" He looked around and was glad to see that at least they all agreed on that, for now.

CHAPTER NINETEEN

She was surprised at how understanding and willing to help Deacon and the others were. She wasn't surprised that they would help in general, but to help her when it was as dangerous as it was tugged at her heart. Deacon had always been protective of her, and she knew the stress he was under knowing that someone was after her.

She went over all the details, starting with the first time that she saw Cami up until that day, and studied each one's expression as she spoke. Avery showed no doubt whatsoever while Deacon and Nick listened stoned faced. She knew they would support her either way, but she had hoped they would actually believe that Cami had appeared to her. She wondered if the only reason she saw Cami was because she believed that it was her. Maybe she can't appear to non-believers. *Listen to yourself. You sound crazy.* She had no way of knowing why or how she appeared, but she did and that was all Carsyn needed to motivate her.

After they listened to everything she had to say, Nick suggested that they go in his truck and that they take it slowly. He wanted them to park away from the area and watch for at least 30 minutes to make sure the area was clear. Everyone agreed and the plans were set.

Carsyn's heart was thumping like the sound of a horse galloping down a street. They had been sitting on the side of the road for almost 20 minutes before a car appeared at the church. They watched as an older gentlemen got out of the car with flowers and walked back to the mausoleum. She wasn't sure her heart could stand waiting 10 more minutes. She was so close to the place she thought Cami to be and wanted to race forward but she had promised to stay calm and stick to the plan.

The church bells started to ring signaling that it was 9am. She glanced at Deacon expecting to see the same smile he always sported when he heard the bells. She was disappointed to see the stern look on his face that indicated he was too distracted to enjoy them. She looked away and focused on the parking lot again. Time was moving so slowly she could almost hear the non-existing ticking of the clock. Deacon's phone rang and everyone jumped to attention. Carsyn could see the caller id and wondered what Detective Stevens had to say.

"Good morning, Detective." Deacon still carried the concerned look on his face. He put the phone on speaker so that everyone could hear the conversation.

"We still don't have a positive identification on the man that broke into the shop last night. My guess is that we won't find anything on him because he's probably an illegal. Same thing for the man that entered your house last night. I do have some connections on the streets, and hope I can find some answers there. These gangs are usually boisterous and callous in their operations. They are not afraid of being caught because they know they will never face consequences thanks to the new laxed laws. They don't even try to hide and are often engaging in criminal activity in broad daylight." Detective Stevens sounded deflated as he spoke.

"What about the pocketknife? I'm guessing that was also a dead end." Carsyn sounded just as deflated as the detective.

"Unfortunately, another dead end but I do have the knife and will continue to follow that lead. Sorry I don't have better news for ya'll. Are ya'll tucked away someplace safe today?"

Deacon started to answer. "We are following…"

Carsyn grabbed his arm and shook her head. She wasn't sure why but didn't want Deacon to tell the Detective what they were up to.

He continued. "We're following instructions and are staying safe. Keep us updated please."

"I will. When I know something you'll be the first to know. Talk to you soon."

Deacon disconnected the call just as Carsyn was getting out of the truck. The phone call was a nice distraction and helped pass the time. They had been sitting in the car for 35 minutes at that point and she was ready to move. She stood up straight but didn't move right away. Every time she saw Cami she was in some kind of trouble. She was terrified that she wouldn't be able to find her or the veil. She had been so sure she would find the veil the last time, but it wasn't there. Not where she had remembered it to be anyway. Deacon must've sensed her apprehension because he came up behind her, put his arm on her back, and nudged her forward. She didn't look at him because she knew if she did she'd break down and she needed to stay strong. She couldn't forget that there was still a threat out there and they needed to be careful.

She felt like her heart skipped a beat with each step. She was approaching the spot where she'd last seen the veil and didn't see anything resembling the beautiful apparition that lured her in the last time. She stopped about ten feet from the spot and shut her eyes. Deacon was right behind her and the other two were not far behind.

Carsyn summoned the memory of her first sight of the veil and concentrated on it hoping to trigger something. She held out both arms and slowly walked a few more feet forward only opening her eyes once she stopped again. She could feel Deacons eyes on her and hoped that he would stay patient. Softly, she launched into the sweet song that meant so much to her family, herself included.

"When I was just a little girl I asked my mother, what will I be? Will I be pretty? Will I be rich? Here's what she said to me. Que sera, sera. Whatever will be will be. The future's not ours to see. Que sera, sera. What will be, will be." After each sentence she hesitated and waited to hear a response then continued to the next.

Carsyn sang louder and louder as she progressed through the song. Her voice shook and her body was stiff as a board while she silently prayed for a miracle. She had never wanted something so badly in her entire life. She wanted to find Cami. She needed to find Cami.

She was at the end of the second verse when she noticed the area around her was getting brighter. She sang louder and prayed harder and then suddenly it appeared. The beautiful veil was just as beautiful and spectacular as she'd remembered. She turned to see if the rest of them could see it and beamed with happiness when she saw the awestruck look on their faces. They see it! They can see it! I'm not crazy! They see it too! Carsyn turned back to face the veil and started to move forward but Deacon grabbed her arm.

"Wait. We don't know what that is. How do you know that Cami's in there? Just because she was the last time doesn't mean she's there now. Let me go first." Deacon pleaded with her to listen to him.

"I love you Deacon. And I love how you always want to protect me, but this is something I have to do. I know you are worried, but Cami won't let anything happen to me. She saved my life when I needed her the most. Please understand that this is something that I have to do." She hated to see the anguish on Deacon's face.

She looked back at Nick and Avery and knew that if anything did happen to her they would be there for Deacon. But she had no doubt that she'd found Cami and that her sister would protect her if needed. She chuckled because she almost finished that thought with 'protect her with her life if needed' but that wasn't accurate. She didn't find anything about the situation funny, but it was certainly ironic. She was depending on her deceased sister to protect her and had refused the help of her husband who was alive and standing beside her. She couldn't explain how she felt and wasn't going to try. He just needed to trust her.

Carsyn took one step at a time and returned to singing as she closed the gap between herself and the veil. She was disappointed that Cami hadn't joined in yet, but she stayed determined to keep singing and to keep going. Finally she stood right in front of the veil of shimmering lights and just basked in the warm feeling of serenity it was projecting. She reached out her hand and the tips of her fingers tingled from the surge of energy it was emitting. Impulsively, she withdrew her hand quickly and rubbed it with the other. Her adrenaline was at peak level, and she felt energized. She knew it was time to dive forward and through the veil to the other side.

She hesitated, not because she was afraid of the veil but because she didn't want Deacon to worry about her. She leaned into him and wrapped her arms around him. She wasn't saying goodbye but instead wanted to reassure him that it was the right choice and that she needed to do it. He grabbed her and pulled her in tightly. He was telling her with his body that he didn't want her to go. She freed from the embrace and turned toward the veil when suddenly something pulled her in, then instantly closed behind her.

CHAPTER TWENTY

Deacon raced after Carsyn but when he reached out to grab her arm, the veil disappeared along with her. He flailed his arms helplessly as he searched for the veil.

"It has to be here. Where did she go? Nick, help me. She was just here."

He looked back and noticed that Nick and Avery were already in frantic mode feeling around and searching for Carsyn and the veil. "

This can't be happening. Where did she go? God please help me. Carsyn! Carsyn! Carsyn where are you?"

Deacon stood still and tried to absorb what had just happened. He thought how ridiculous all of this seemed and felt like there had to be a reasonable explanation. He believed Carsyn when she said she saw Cami but deep down had his doubts. "Cami! Where's Cami? Did either of you see Cami? If the veil was here Cami must be close by. God, I hope she's with Carsyn. She has to be. None of this makes sense." Deacon ran his fingers through his hair and leaned over to catch his breath.

Before anyone answered, he started to shout for Cami again.

"Cami! Cami! Please Cami! Carsyn needs you! Are you here? Please!" His voice cracked as he spoke his last word.

His hands slid down from his hair and covered his eyes that were glistening from his feeling of helplessness. After a few moments he regained control and lowered his hands to his cheeks and noticed the mystified looks on both Nick and Avery's faces. He spun around and there just a few feet in front of him was Cami just as young and beautiful as the day she died.

He lunged forward to hug her but instead crossed through her body and landed on the ground. He scrambled to his feet getting back in front of her.

"Cami. How is this possible? How are you here?" The urgency in his voice faded and his words sounded curious instead.

CHAPTER TWENTY-ONE

Carsyn was confused. In a matter of seconds, she was thrust into a world she knew nothing about. What was she supposed to do?

"No! Wait! I wasn't ready! What happened to the veil? Where am I?" She urgently reached for the veil and felt around the area, but it was gone. The veil was gone. Deacon, Avery, and Nick were gone. She was all alone in an unfamiliar place. She flopped to the ground and started to weep because she didn't know what was happening or what she was supposed to do. The only thing she knew was that she needed her sister now more than ever. Cami? Are you here? She sat still and listened for a moment before starting to whisper her song again.

"When I was just a little girl, I asked my mother what will I be? Will I be pretty will I be rich, here's what she said to me. Que sera sera. Whatever will be, will be..." She waited for Cami to join in, but she never did.

Scared, and frustrated, Carsyn stood up, dusted herself off and looked around. The first thing she noticed was the soft sunlight that seemed to radiate from as far as she could see. There were hills and trees and yellow wildflowers that covered the lush green ground. She listened carefully and could hear movement of water, possibly a stream or a small waterfall, not too far away. She could hear the birds chirping in the distance and the sweet smell of flowers tickled her nose. A sense of familiarity struck her, and she began to feel at ease.

Further in the distance, a burst of light caught her attention followed by a low rumble that reminded her of the sounds of an afternoon thunderstorm approaching. She leaned forward readjusting her vision just in time for the next burst of light but this time it appeared closer. The low rumble also sounded louder as time progressed and was joined by a sound she wasn't familiar with. Her momentary feeling of ease was replaced with a rush of fear of the unknown.

She looked around for a place to take cover. She thought back to when she was there with Cami but was unable to recall anything about the area. She was too busy accepting the fact that she was having a conversation with her deceased sister to be concerned with her surroundings. Am I even in the veil? Everything happened so quickly that she couldn't even recall weather or not she had finally found the veil. She wondered what Deacon and the others were thinking and was sure they were looking to find her. They had to be just as confused as she was.

As the sky darkened and the wind picked up, the landscape transformed to display a much scarier picture. The peaceful serene place she originally landed in was slowly disappearing and it reminded her of the "Wizard of Oz" when Dorothy said, "We're not in Kansas anymore, To-

to." She had no idea where she was, but she knew for certain that she was no longer in Crown Point.

The trees and lush lawn were also changing, and she could feel a light mist on her arms. Carsyn backed up slowly until she reached the closest tree never losing sight of what was happening in front of her. She moved to the back of the tree and squatted down close to the ground. She listened as the unfamiliar sound grew louder and decided that it sounded like a stampede. She was reminded of another movie "Jumanji" when the herd of animals were running down the street. Her nervous laugh was low but faded away quickly.

Her vison started to become compromised by an enormous wall of dust that was rolling in like fog, but it wasn't empty. There was something or someone moving with the dust that was headed her way. Panic took over and all she could do was stay crouched down, cover her face, and scream.

"Cami! Cami! Please Cami, I need you. I'm scared. Hurry. I don't know what's happening. Cami!" Reluctantly, she spread her fingers just enough to get a peak. Standing right in front of her face was a horrifying black skeleton looking creature with big sharp teeth. She dropped her hands and let out the loudest blood curdling scream before everything went completely black. The dust was so thick that she couldn't see her hands in front of her face. All she managed to do was whisper, "Cami please" before the dust filled air took her breath away.

She felt her body depleting from lack of oxygen and instead of fighting it just surrendered to the feeling. Her life started to flash before her eyes just like she'd heard it did right before death. The first memories to appear were of her mother and father. The corners of her mouth slanted upward as the tender moments raced across her mind and warmed her heart. Unfortunately, the memories of the death of her parents came to pass and brought with it the same feeling of dread she felt when it happened. Thankfully, like a movie reel playing in a theater, the memories moved forward and landed on Cami and the happiness and closeness they'd shared. Alarm set in when she realized that she was going to have to relive Cami's death all over again. I can't! I won't! Please no! She had no idea how to stop the memories, but she knew she had to do something. She tried to open her eyes, but the dust was pounding even harder, and she felt hopeless until she felt someone grip her arm. Her body jolted from the surprise, but then her mind kicked into gear, and she reached out with both of her hands to grab onto her only salvation.

"I'm here baby sister! I'm here. Hold on." Cami pulled Carsyn away from the tree and into a protected embrace. "I got you just hold on."

A tear formed in Carsyn's eye when she realized it was her sister that came for her and that she was no longer alone, but the wind and dust was so fierce, it dried up before it had a chance to escape. She squeezed her eyes tighter and held on for dear life. Cami was there and she was going to protect her like always.

The dust storm appeared quickly and ended just as fast. When Carsyn reopened her eyes the sky had grown light again, and the sweet smell of flowers had returned. She refused to let go of Cami in fear of everything changing again. She felt like she was losing her mind and wasn't sure how much more of the craziness she could take. At least in Cami's arms she felt protected and safe and a bit invincible. That wasn't the case just a few moments ago when she felt like her life was over. After a reasonable amount of time passed she allowed Cami to loosen her grip and release her from the embrace.

"What happened? Where were you? I was so scared. Did you see those things? They looked like the creatures from the movie The Mummy with Brendan Fraser. I swear I thought I was gonna see him jump out and fight the creatures. The dust rolled in so quickly that I couldn't see anything. Did you see that thing? I heard it coming, the dust. It sounded like that scene from "Jumanji." Do you remember when we watched that movie? That was crazy." Carsyn was rambling on and on about her experience.

"Are you insane? What is wrong with you?" Cami was staring at her sister in disbelief.

Carsyn stopped rattling on and gave Cami a puzzled look. "What's wrong with you?"

"What's wrong with me? We are in an unknown dangerous place with bizarre things happening all around us and you're going on about movies!"

"What do you mean unknown? This is where you live now, right? It's known to you, right Cami?" Worry was beginning to creep into Carsyn's mind.

"What do you mean? I don't live here. I don't know anything about this place."

"Sure you do. I called out for you, and you were here." She watched for some understanding in her sister's face. She hoped for a sign of agreement that they were safe now. It didn't come. "Cami, tell me you know where we are, please." Carsyn was tired and dreaded what was to come.

"Listen, I have no idea where we are. I thought you understood that. All I know is that you called out for me, and I heard you." Cami's forehead wrinkled with concern. "I don't know where I live now. The only thing I ever remember is when I'm with you." With a twisted expression she went on. "Why do you think that is? Do you think there's some kind of block on our memories when we die so that it remains a mystery? That has to be it because I don't remember anything else." The concern only grew as she sorted through things and realized that she had no recollection of her afterlife. Fear slipped into her mind because of all the unanswered questions, and she suddenly felt frail and useless.

Carsyn noticed the slight tremble in Cami's voice as she spoke the last few words and her heart felt shattered for her sister. How could she not remember being dead? What was it like for her on the other side? Like Cami, she had so many questions that she knew would never be answered.

Cami noticed the pity in her sister's eyes and sprang into action. "We have to go now." She tugged on Carsyn's arm urging her to follow. She may not remember too much but she did know that she was there to protect her sister and that was what she was going to do. They ran toward a dim light that was in the opposite direction from where they were. She wrapped her arms around her sister again and watched as the dust storm started to rage again. From inside the storm, scary skeleton men emerged and were charging after them.

"See, just like in the movie "The Mummy." I told you. Do you…" Before she finished her sentence, Cami leaped forward with her in tow and crashed through the lighted wall that had grown brighter lighting the way. In unison they screamed and prayed at the same time. She wasn't sure where they were gonna end up, but it had to be better than staying there with 'The Mummy' monsters.

CHAPTER TWENTY-TWO

Deacon was still adapting to the fact that his wife's dead sister had appeared right in front of him when, just as quickly as she appeared, she disappeared.

"Wait! Cami, come back! We need you! Carsyn needs you!" He looked at Avery and Nick for answers but knew they were just as confused as he was.

"Where'd she go? CAMI! This can't be happening." Deacon covered his face and screamed. "Ugh! My God, Carsyn where are you? Avery, do you remember exactly where she saw the veil? It was right here wasn't it? She kept saying it was right here the last time but was frantic when she couldn't find it. Right? Everything happened so quickly, and she was disappointed that it wasn't here. It reappeared and then she was gone. And where did Cami disappear to? I didn't have time to tell her that Carsyn needed her. I didn't have time!" Deacon was now spiraling out of control.

"Slow down brother." Nick grabbed Deacon's arm and tried to reason with him. "We're gonna find her but you need to get a grip. Carsyn said that Cami always shows up when she's in trouble so maybe that's where she disappeared to. It has to be." Nick was concerned about Deacon who was pale as a ghost.

"Let's sit down and talk about what just happened. Panicking won't do us any good." Avery sat down on a bench.

Deacon paced for a few more seconds before having a seat next to Avery to possibly find out what she knew about this situation. Carsyn had told him that she confided in Avery first, and since she just told him about seeing Cami that morning, maybe Avery had more information to share.

"Did Carsyn say anything else about Cami or the Veil? Did she say she knew how to contact Cami because I was under the impression that she just randomly appeared." Deacon stood up again and continued to pace.

"No. She didn't know how to contact her. She did say that usually she was singing that song she loves so much, Que Sera Sera. She mentioned that it was special to both of them and their mother. Deacon, this was the first time I actually saw Cami. The other times Carsyn saw her but all I saw was a sudden gust of wind or felt a change in temperature. I was skeptical of course but I did believe that Carsyn believed she was seeing Cami. She didn't talk much about the veil other than she believed that it was an old Irish belief that in sacred places, our world and the after world were only a few feet apart. Do you think this is a sacred place, right here in Crown Point? The last time she went into the veil, it was Cami that pulled her in but we saw Cami after Carsyn disappeared so it couldn't have been her this time." Avery rubbed at the goosebumps that covered her arms. She wished she would've kept that last thought to herself because she noticed the impact it had on Deacon.

"What are we going to do? We can't call the police, what would we say? Hi, my wife disappeared into thin air and I'm afraid that she may be trapped in another world. They would lock me up for sure. But we can't just sit here. Let's spread out and see if we can find this doorway or curtain or whatever you want to call it. We can't just leave her in there." Deacon didn't wait for a response but instead set out toward the last place he saw his wife.

He was growing angrier as time passed. He wasn't angry at Carsyn but instead at himself for not protecting her. Was she afraid to approach him with the truth about Cami's appearance? He had always tried to be open and supportive, especially in the last few years, but did he fail her? He was supposed to protect her and keep her safe and the last few days proved that he wasn't doing a good job. She was carjacked, shot, left for dead, stalked, and attacked again at the shop and now lost in a world in which she didn't belong. The overwhelming guilt he felt welled up into his throat as he tried to make sense of it all.

The time seemed to crawl by and even though it'd only been a few minutes since she disappeared, it felt like an eternity. Eternity. Ironic that that word popped into his mind. He wasn't sure what he believed about eternity, but the current events have shaken him to his core. How was it possible that Cami appeared to them? Was she left in limbo out there waiting to move on? That thought was unnerving, and he literally shook his body in an attempt to shake off that feeling of dread and doom, a subject no one likes to think about.

He'd heard of people seeing ghosts and spirits, but he never really paid attention to any of it and usually dismissed it as nonsense. He still questioned the vision of Cami that was floating right in front of him just minutes ago. If Nick and Avery hadn't been with him and witnessed the same thing, he would've thought he was going crazy or at the very least hallucinating. But, for reasons unknown, it was really Cami that he saw and in that one experience, his whole world had turned upside down.

His thoughts were all over the place jumping from ghost to Carsyn and back again. He was so absorbed in his own thoughts that when his phone rang, he let out a quick squeal before answering. He quickly recognized that it was a sales call and terminated the call. Complete frustration set in and instead of accepting that the rudeness and inopportune time of sales calls were a part of every day, he swore at his phone and was tempted to throw it across the parking lot.

The surprised look on Avery's face told him that his behavior was unacceptable and that it wouldn't do anyone any good, especially Carsyn. He inhaled deeply and refocused. He was beating himself up because he knew he was out of ideas and certainly not equipped to deal with the peculiar situation.

Avery spoke up the minute a helpful thought occurred to her.

"I'm not sure how helpful this will be, but I remember Carsyn telling me she wanted to call Fr. Terry about the Irish traditions and folklores. She thought since he was from Ireland maybe he would know some way to contact Cami. I know it's a longshot but if Carsyn thought he could help her, maybe he can help us now."

Deacon didn't even respond but instead hit contacts on his phone and dialed Fr. Terry's number. Why hadn't he thought of that? With all that had happened, he was not thinking straight, and worried that was going to dampen his chances in finding Carsyn.

"It went straight to voicemail, but I left him a message that it was urgent that I speak with him. Thanks Avery, that was a good idea."

"Don't thank me, it was your wife's idea. I just re-called the conversation and to be honest I'm sorry I didn't think of it sooner." Avery had been trying to recall every-thing, big and small, that she and Carsyn had discussed just in case it triggered something important.

They walked back to the truck to regroup and get a drink of water. The weather wasn't that bad, but it was hot enough to add to the stress that was already present. It was the humidity that was so oppressive, and even though they were born and raised in the area, it was taking a toll on their energy and ability to focus.

Deacon's phone rang at the same time a loud crashing noise came from the edge of the woods. All three of them ran in the direction of the noise and into the cover of the woods exactly where just a day ago held the body of a women barely alive. Deacon was the first one to enter and was not prepared for what he saw lying on the ground just a few feet in front of him.

"Oh my God!"

CHAPTER TWENTY-THREE

Carsyn was growing tired of getting banged up and thrown around. Her body was already achy and bruised and now she was sure she could add broken bones to the list. Cami could've given her a heads up but instead she grabbed her and dove through the veil, or so that's what she hoped it was. When they emerged on the other side they landed hard on the ground in a wooded area. Cami jumped up quickly looking back in the direction they came from ready to attack.

Carsyn stayed on the ground clutching her shoulder and catching her breath. She watched her sister in amusement. "What are you doing? You look ridiculous." She suddenly sat up keeping her eyes on her. "Wait, do you think those things can follow us through the veil? Cami, do you think they can do that?"

"I have no idea. How would I know? This is all new to me too. I told you I don't have any memories except my time with you, but we need to be ready just in case." She continued to stand on guard waiting for an attack.

"I still can't understand that. You've been gone for a few years now, what were you doing all that time? You should've at least discovered what you could and couldn't do, like fly, walk through walls, and appear to people. You were always the smart one in the family, what happened?"

"There are no words for you!" Cami dismissed Carsyn and moved on trying to figure out where they were.

"Gee, what's wrong with you? I just think that it would be really helpful right now if you had learned something about being dead."

"Can you walk?" She helped Carsyn up hoping she was alright.

"I think so. I hurt my shoulder again but everything else seems okay, just a little sore." She reached down to her wounded leg to check for bleeding. "Do you know where we are? It looks kind of familiar to me like I've been here before. Did you hear that?"

Cami raised her finger to her lips to silence Carsyn who immediately shut up. She heard branches cracking as someone was making their way toward them.

Cami mouthed the words to Carsyn. "We have to move, now."

She put her arm around Cami's shoulder, and they quietly made their way away from the noise. She wondered why they were running away from potential help but figured that it was because of all the danger they'd faced the last few days. *Does Cami think that it could be the men that assaulted me?* She felt a surge of adrenaline shoot through her body giving her the strength to move faster just in case the sound came from an unwanted intruder like her attackers.

Once they were far enough into the woods they found a few fallen trees to take cover. Everything looked familiar but at the same time different. The trees seemed bigger and more intrusive while the ground was covered with roots and vines which made it difficult to move through quickly. The air had a thickness to it almost as if it were alive and pushing against her. She cradled closer to her sister looking for safety and security.

"I don't think we are back in Crown Point. Do you suppose it's possible that we landed someplace else? Oh I forgot; you don't remember." Carsyn squeezed her sister tighter. "I'm sorry if I've been difficult, and no matter what happens, I want you to know that I have never stopped loving you and I am so happy that you're here. After you left, my whole world was turned upside down. I love my husband and he was supportive and amazing but the hole in my heart never healed." Carsyn had begun to cry. "There are so many wonderful loving people in my life that were there for me, but no one could replace you Cami. I watch other people enjoy their lives with their sisters and while that makes me happy for them it saddens me at the same time. For the longest I questioned my faith and my reason for living. You were such a faithful, loving person, not only to God but to everyone you met, so much more than me, so why you? Why did he take you? It's not fair!"

Cami was so touched she was speechless for a moment.

"I can't begin to imagine what you went through. If it had been you, I would not have survived. Since our parents died, especially mom since she went first, you were my world, and I was yours. And like you, I loved my husband but the bond you and I shared was special. Apparently, unbreakable because here I am." Cami was crying too, something she wasn't sure she was still capable of feeling considering the circumstances.

They both sat there in silence holding on to each other for support and comfort. Carsyn hadn't felt that secure in years. That unconditional love she'd always felt from her sister was back and was covering her like a warm blanket on a cold day. Her heart felt like it was going to explode from the joy she was feeling. It didn't take long for the idea that she would probably have to face losing Cami all over again, to invade her mind and hijack her peace.

Cami tried to release from their embrace, but Carsyn tightened her grip. "Just a few more minutes, please. I just want to stay like this forever, but I know we have to get back to reality soon. Things have been in such an uproar for a few days, no, actually a few years would be more accurate, and it just feels so good to be able to enjoy the calm."

Naturally, the outside world forced its way in again and her moment was disrupted by the sound of someone or something approaching. She released Cami from their embrace and waited to see who was sharing the woods with them and was most likely searching for them. They remained hidden because the intruders were now right above them,

"Carsyn! Cami!" Deacon's voice traveled throughout the woods coming from their right.

Carsyn started to respond, but Cami covered her mouth and made eye contact telling her to be quiet. The noise from the approaching footsteps increased but was now going in the opposite direction of Deacon's voice and away from them. They waited until the sound faded away and stood up. Cami still motioned for Carsyn to keep quiet as they tried to regain strength in their legs. She was surprised just how wobbly she felt but noticed that the eerie appearance of the woods was slowly improving as the sounds of Deacon and her family moved in closer. Once they were sure the threat was far enough away, she called out to Deacon and before she realized it, Cami was gone, again. The last thing she said was, "I never left you, I had no choice in the matter."

CHAPTER TWENTY-FOUR

Each time Cami disappeared, Carsyn prayed that she would be able to find her again. The separation still initially ripped her heart open, but optimism that she would see her again replaced the helpless feeling and allowed her to keep from completely falling apart.

Deacon was almost upon her so she climbed over the fallen trees and out into the open so that he could see her. *I guess we did land in Crown Point after all.* Her heart soared at the sight of her husband.

"Baby, what happened?" Deacon raced to his wife and threw his arms around her. He noticed how she flinched when he squeezed her tightly. "Are you alright? Did you hurt yourself again?"

Subconsciously, she reached for her shoulder and was reminded that she hurt it when she and Cami jumped back through the veil. *How did I go through the veil in the first place? It wasn't Cami this time because she wasn't there.* She hadn't thought about that until this moment.

"I hurt my shoulder when we jumped back through the veil." She looked around and this time recognized exactly where she was. The area seemed to have transformed completely from when they first fell to the ground. She didn't have an explanation as to why, or how that would occur. Heck, she didn't have an explanation for any of the bizarre events she had encountered recently either.

Avery, along with Nick, finally reached them and she expressed her relief at having found her safe. She saw the disappointment in Carsyn's eyes and knew that it was there for Cami. "I'm glad you're alright. You scared us to death. The moment you found the veil both you and the veil were gone."

"I don't know. I didn't see anything but felt a force pull me forward. The next thing I knew, I was standing in an unknown area all alone. At first I thought it was Cami that pulled me through, but it wasn't, and the place turned really dark and scary. There were even monsters this time." Carsyn stopped after that last statement because she was sure they would think she was crazy.

"Sweetheart, we saw Cami. She appeared to us right after you disappeared. I called out for her, and she came but she quickly disappeared. Did you see her? Did she find you?"

"What?" She heard the words that came out of Deacon's mouth, but they didn't register at first.

"We saw Cami." Avery stepped forward and reached for her hand. "She came when you were in trouble just like you said. Seeing her was so incredible but also unbelievable. Carsyn, she came for you."

She stared into Deacon's eyes with disbelief. "You saw her? You believe me?" She wrapped her arms around Deacon and just exhaled in relief.

Her heart silently soared with happiness because she no longer felt alone. She knew that Avery wanted to believe, and probably did to some degree, but witnessing it for herself left no questions. Well, no questions about the actual appearance of Cami but there were plenty of questions surrounding the phenomenon. They all had questions just as she did, but unfortunately, she wasn't sure they were going to find any answers any time soon.

She was elated to have her family's support and was truly grateful, but there was a side of her that was still devasted about Cami. For years now, she'd put up a front and acted like she had accepted that her sister was gone and had worked through her feelings, however, that was far from the truth. Carsyn's loss of her sister was with her every minute of every day and threatened to take over and destroy her at any moment. She hated seeing the pain her grief had caused Deacon and the others, so she fought to be strong and often pretended that she was alright.

They couldn't have been any more supportive, but at the same time they couldn't relate to her pain, and she recognized that. She was grateful that none of them had to endure the pain she felt and also knew that they would understand had she expressed that to them. This was something that she had to work through alone. She felt abandoned and scared at times. Even in a house full of people, people she loved and adored, she felt alone and lost without Cami. She'd also believed that time would help her heal, but she was still waiting for that to happen. The vulnerable rawness that she felt had her emotions in a tailspin all the time and she hated that out of control feeling. A part of her died with her sister.

With Deacon's help, she walked back to the truck, climbed in the passenger side, and slid into the middle to rest her head on Deacon's shoulder. She felt exhausted.

"Hey, how long was I gone?" She wondered if time was the same on both sides.

"Maybe about ten minutes or so. It seemed like eternity on our side, what about for you?" Deacon involuntarily shuddered at the reminder of frantically looking for her when she vanished.

She was deep in thought again as she replayed what had happened in her mind. She too felt like it was an eternity but at the same time admitted that it was about the same. That's one of the many questions that she'd wondered about. But why does Cami still look the same as she did when she passed?

"You said ya'll saw Cami, why do you think she looks the same as if no time had passed at all for her? She told me that she doesn't have any memory of anything except her time with me." As she tossed that concept around she remembered that when the skeleton monsters were getting closer Cami knew exactly where to jump through the veil that until then had been invisible. She must know things, but maybe that knowledge doesn't cross over with her.

The drive back to the rental was quiet. The more she searched for Cami the crazier things got, but she didn't care. She would never stop her search. Sooner or later, she was going to find answers and figure out a way to keep her sister in her life. She knew that fact was what was bothering Deacon and had him in deep thought. Carsyn watched as they were all trying to come to terms with their new knowledge of Cami and the afterlife in their own way. She on the other hand was thinking about the tattoo that was on her attackers wrist and wondered if it was done locally.

The thought of going back to the rental and sitting there all day made her feel anxious. She couldn't just sit around and wait for that detective to do something because there was something about him that rubbed her the wrong way. Not that she didn't trust him, but he didn't seem to be too anxious to find answers and she wanted some quickly. *Really, how long does it take to get results from the government tattoo recognition system? They probably have a match and are waiting for him to check in with them. I bet he didn't even visit the local tattoo shops. That was a really good clue I gave him. I should go to the shops myself and see what I can find out.* She knew there were a few on Manhattan Blvd in Harvey but didn't know how to convince her husband to go there.

"I don't know about ya'll, but I don't want to go back to the rental and sit there all afternoon. Can we please at least get something to eat? Before you say no, think about it. How long do we sit and wait? What if a few days turn into weeks or months? We can wear hats and blend in with the others." That last statement softened the mood and even made everyone laugh a little.

"Alright. Alright. We can go but we need a different vehicle to drive around. I'll call Detective Stevens and see if he can help us out." Deacon hated to admit it, but Carsyn was right. They needed to be proactive or else they may be in hiding for a while.

"No! Don't call him. We can call an uber. Or better yet, maybe we can uber to a rental car place and rent a truck for the week. That way we'll have transportation if we need it, and no one will know what we're driving." She thought that was a brilliant idea and she just hoped they'd agree because she wanted to get to those tattoo parlors soon.

CHAPTER TWENTY-FIVE

After stopping to change clothes, and put on 'hats and disguises' as Nick kept calling it, they called an uber and went to the car rental place. They decided on a truck and before long they were headed to Gattuso's Restaurant in Gretna, which was conveniently close to several local tattoo shop. There seemed to be plenty shops, and she was confident that one of them would recognize the particular tattoo for which she was searching. *They have to.* Surprisingly, the others agreed so they headed to the closest one.

Her hair was in a ponytail and tucked into her hat. She felt a little silly, but it made Deacon relax and that was worth it to her. She thought about what she was going to say when she walked into the shop. She had friends that had tattoos, but she and Deacon didn't have any. She knew that Avery didn't have any and was most certain that Nick didn't either, but she wasn't sure about that. Maybe they could pretend that they wanted to get their first tattoos together but wasn't sure exactly what kind they wanted.

Carsyn was surprised to see how clean and bright the shop was. That was her first time inside a tattoo shop, and she didn't know what to expect. The only pictures she had in her mind were the ones she'd seen on television shows, and they were all portrayed as small, dark and smokey. The young man closest to the entrance was busy working on a client and didn't look up. After a few moments he told them to take a seat and yelled to the back for some assistance.

Carsyn's mouth dropped open when a tall, dark, and handsome man walked into the room. He had long hair wrapped up in a man bun and by the shape of his body, he worked out regularly. Surprisingly, his arms were bare, no tattoos. It wasn't that he was gorgeous that shocked her but that he was completely opposite from what she'd expected to see there. She quickly recovered and wondered if he was tattoo free or just preferred to get them where the public couldn't see.

"Hello. I'm Levi. What can I do for you?"

Deacon spoke up first. "We were thinking about getting matching tattoo's to celebrate our anniversary." He wrapped his arm around Carsyn and smiled at Levi.

"Sure mate. What did you have in mind?" He waited for one of them to respond.

"I was thinking about a cross. Do you have any books we can look through of your prior work?" She'd hoped he did.

"I think we have a few pictures laying around the place. Of course those on the wall are the most popular.

We can do anything you want if you have a picture." He spoke as he fished through a mess of pictures on a table.

There was muffled noise coming from the back of the shop. When she tried to walk closer to the hallway leading to the back, Levi stepped out in front of her blocking her view and that triggered a red flag.

"Can I use your restroom?" Her eyes met his.

"Sorry love, it's out of order. The station across the street should have accommodations." He flashed a smile at her.

His accent threw her off but something about him was sending bad vibes and she always believed in paying attention to them no matter the circumstance. She looked at the others who were waiting for her next move. Clearly, they were not getting tattoos so at one point they had to tuck tail and leave. She walked back over to the table and picked up some of the pictures to look through. She started to hum her song trying to stay calm and patient. She really wanted to know what he was hiding in the back but that wasn't going to be easy. She motioned for the others to look through all the pictures in search of the cross. At least when they left, they would know that it wasn't offered at that shop or at least not to everyone.

They searched every picture they could find and while there were plenty of crosses, none matched the tattoos on her assailants wrists. The cross she was looking for was more of a Celtic cross with a circle in the middle. She referred to it as Celtic because of the research she'd done last night. She was still disappointed in the little information she found on Irish folklore and Veils. She couldn't completely blame the internet because her googling skills were not the best. Usually, she would reach out to Avery or her friend Charisse when she needed help but under the circumstances, she hadn't had time. Maybe she'll give Charisse a call later.

Carsyn was determined to find that tattoo so she walked back to Levi to see if he could direct her in the right direction. Something about him caused her concern but she didn't know why. She suspected that Levi wasn't his real name but decided not to push that issue. Instead she would try to get his help by pretending to be nice and most of all naive. He looked like someone that would appreciate a women in need and try to help her.

"Hey Levi, can you help me please? As you can see this is the first time we're getting tattoos, and we really have our hearts set on a particular cross. You see my mother-n-laws family is Irish and we want to get a certain cross that his grandmother used to have." Carsyn reached for her phone and pulled up the cropped picture from her ring camera of the man's wrist as he entered her house. She cropped out the name but left the rest of the Celtic cross. "I'm not even sure it could be tattooed as small as I would want it to be. What do you think? I want to get it on my wrist but again, I just want it to be tiny."

She watched as his jaw tightened and his friendly demeanor changed. He looked at the picture for a few seconds longer then looked her straight in the eyes. He smiled and said, "Sorry, love. I can't help you. There's a lot of detail to that picture and I'm afraid it wouldn't look good so small. Maybe you'd like a nice heart instead." As he spoke his last words, he was already walking back to the front desk where there were pictures of hearts.

Carsyn followed him determined to continue their conversation. She watched as the other man in the shop never looked up and just continued working on his current canvas. She didn't want to interrupt him, but maybe he would be more helpful. Before she could make up her mind, Levi interrupted.

"I wish I could help you, but I really think you'd be disappointed if you tried to get that tattoo so small." His warm friendly demeanor returned.

"Maybe you're right. But do you have any pictures of a Celtic Cross that was done here before? My husband and brother n law may still want one."

Levi shook his head no and while he appeared to want to say more, he decided not to.

"Can you at least point us in another direction. Maybe another shop that might be able to help us?" Carsyn was growing impatient.

"Sorry. I'm new to the area. Jared over there has been here a while, but we can't disturb him right now. How about you come back tomorrow afternoon and talk to him then? Hopefully, he can help you find what you are looking for." He glanced at his watch. "Besides we're closing soon for lunch, and I really need to get things done before we leave." He walked from behind the desk and ushered them out the door, waved goodbye and locked it behind them. He even pulled down the shade and turned off the open sign that hung flashing in the window.

Carsyn looked at the sign on the door that provided the store hours. The shop was open seven days a week from 10 to 10. It didn't list closing for lunch but maybe that's something new. Since covid, most businesses were having trouble finding people to work so maybe they were short-handed and had to close for lunch. She wasn't sure she believed that, but she had to accept that she hit a dead end there and had to move on. She looked at her phone and hoped that the picture she'd snapped of Levi had come out clear. She was pleased to see that it had and while she had her phone out, she searched google for other tattoo parlors in the area.

Nick spoke up first. "This is crazy. What are we going to do if we find the tattoo parlor that did that tattoo? We can't trust they will give us any information about their clients. Besides, I know Levi looked okay, but did you see the other guy? He looked a little rough and he never once smiled when he looked up. I have to believe that there's some sort of code they go by to protect themselves and their clients. We have to be careful. And what if we find the information we want, what are we going to do with it? Carsyn, I'm not trying to discourage you, but I know we all have to be thinking these same thoughts."

Carsyn smiled at Nick. She reached out and grabbed his hand. "Hey. I know you are right, and I know you are trying to help me. Thank you. Really, thanks for your love and support." She backed up and addressed all of them. "I know you are all trying to help, and I would like to take a moment to say how important ya'll are to me and how grateful I am. I know this is crazy and I know it's dangerous, but I don't know what else to do. I hadn't said anything, but I don't trust that detective. I don't have anything to validate my feelings except my gut telling me not to trust him. And if I'm right, there's no one else out there helping us find these men. If any of you have an idea which way we should turn from here, I'm willing to listen. I'm just afraid we are on our own to face these extremely dangerous men and that scares me."

Deacon put his arm around her shoulder and kissed the top of her head. They were all exhausted, emotional, and unsure what their next move should be. Without any other clear plan, they decided to continue to visit more tattoo shops. They'll just figure out what to do when and if they find the right one.

CHAPTER TWENTY-SIX

They had a short drive to the next tattoo shop, so they all took the time to reflect on the situation and tried to come up with a good plan. Carsyn stared out the window and focused on the first shop they visited, more importantly on Levi. He didn't seem like the type of man to work in a tattoo parlor, but she didn't have any experience to compare it to. She just assumed that all tattoo artists would be full of tattoos but that's just prejudice. She chuckled to herself because she felt like she was the most openminded person of everyone she knew and didn't usually judge people. Not that she was judging him, but she had certainly assumed that he didn't fit in with the way society viewed tattoo artists. She also remembered the little tightness of his jaw when he saw the picture of the tattoo on her phone. She could tell that he recognized the tattoo even if he wasn't the one that put it there. She made a mental note to revisit those thoughts and to learn more about that shop and its employees.

She closed her eyes for a brief second and Cami's face appeared. Her expression was hard, and her eyes were filled with sorrow. Carsyn's eyes sprung open, and she gasped for air. She looked around and was relieved to see that no one noticed her behavior. She wasn't trying to hide anything, but she was tired of trying to explain things she didn't even understand herself. Since she was carjacked, she hadn't had any time to herself. She was grateful for the emotional support and definitely didn't want to be alone, but she also needed some quiet time to regroup.

From the start, 'carjacked' was the reason they all accepted for what had happened to her but why would her 'carjackers' still be after her if they only wanted her car? There had to be more to it, but she didn't know what that could be. They must think she could identify them but even that wouldn't warrant the all-out assault they had launched to find her. It seemed a little over the top to go to her house and shop with guns blazing just to stop her from identifying them. *What could they want from me?* Carsyn's mind was tired and the events from the past few days were starting to get all jumbled together and she was no closer to getting answers.

After a brief break, her mind landed on Detective Stevens. She couldn't put her finger on it, but she had a strange feeling he shouldn't be trusted. Maybe he was just lazy, or maybe he was on the take. She realized that over the past few years, the job of a law enforcement officer had become strained and tested at every level, making it difficult for them to do their job and keep themselves and local residents safe. She remembered that he'd slid something in his pocket as the paramedics and police were working to secure the scene, but that could've been any-thing. She wanted to trust him. She needed to trust him, but wasn't sure she could. The only people she trusted at that moment were the people inside that car with her and Cami of course. Most of all Cami.

As the truck stopped she was suddenly brought back to reality. They were in front of another tattoo shop that looked smaller than the last one. She was slow to get up and when she reached for the door, Deacon covered her hand with his.

"You look exhausted. Let me and Nick go in and look around. Send me the picture of the tattoo and I'll ask if they are familiar with it." Deacon knew she was about to object, so he tightened his grip and with his eyes, pleaded that she listen to him.

She did. She removed her hand from the door handle and rubbed her forehead. She waited as he kissed her check, got out, and shut the door behind him. She wasn't alone because Avery stayed in the car with her. Carsyn knew that she had not lost her ability to reason.

"Do you need some time alone or do you want me to stay with you? You won't hurt my feelings either way, but I don't think it's safe for you to be by yourself."

Carsyn leaned forward and put her hand on Avery's shoulder. "Thank you for asking. I'm okay. It's just been a lot to absorb for all of us. I feel like I need quiet time, but I agree sadly it's not really safe right now."

The two men were in the tattoo parlor for about fifteen minutes before they came back out to the truck. By the look on their faces, they had hit another dead end.

"I know this is completely out there but who wants to go to the movies? I sure could use a distraction and some down time. Maybe even a nap." Deacon looked at the rest of them and laughed.

"That sounds good to me. A few distracted hours is exactly what I think we need." Nick started the truck and put it in drive.

Both Carsyn and Avery agreed so they headed up the street to the theatre. They were all acutely aware of their surroundings watching out for any suspicious behavior. On several occasions they saw a white van that seemed to have triggered panic but so far had turned out to be false alarms. Instead of everyone waiting outside for tickets, Nick got in line as the others went into the lobby to wait. They were trying to be as vigilant as they could to stay safe.

Carsyn found it amusing how something could make you so paranoid. Even in the darkness of the movie theatre she was on edge. She was aware of every person that entered and kept an eye on their whereabouts at all times. The movie was halfway over, and she had no idea about what was going on. She tried to pay attention, but scary thoughts kept creeping in and the people around her wouldn't just sit down and enjoy the movie. She looked over at the others and they seemed to be relaxed, in fact, Deacon dozed in and out just as he promised. She was caught up in one of her thoughts when the lights came on and people started to exit the theatre.

Carsyn stood up and when she looked toward the exit she could swear she saw the man from the tattoo parlor, Levi. She scrambled down the steps hoping to catch up with him. Before she reached the bottom, a hand grabbed her from behind and she stopped.

"Whoa Carsyn. Where are you going? You need to wait for us." Deacon had her wrist as he tried to keep up.

She turned out of instinct toward Deacon's voice and when she looked back toward the exit, the man in question was gone.

"I thought I saw Levi leaving the theatre." Carsyn pointed toward the exit and Deacon took off in that direction leaving her behind.

Nick ran after him without knowing what was going on. She explained the situation to Avery as the two of them rushed after them. Once outside, the parking lot was full of people coming out of the movie. She spotted Nick but couldn't find Deacon. After a few minutes, Deacon came from around the side of the building looking upset.

"It was definitely Levi. I spotted him just as he was leaving the parking lot. I tried to catch him, but I was too late. What was he doing here? Do you think he followed us? He would've had to follow us to the other tattoo parlor first." His voice was quick and winded. "It has to be a coincidence, right?"

"I don't know but I say we go find out." Nick had the keys in his hand ready to go.

They jumped in the truck and headed back to the tattoo shop. It was well past the hour they should've closed for lunch. They parked across the street and waited to see if there was any activity coming in or out of the shop. Carsyn hoped that they would catch Levi driving up since he had left just before they did. After some time had passed, Deacon got out and walked across the street and looked into the shop. He waved for Nick to come behind him and then stepped inside the door.

The same guy, Jared, from earlier was there but this time he sat behind the counter flipping through his phone. He looked up for a second then proceeded to look through his phone. "Can I help you?"

Deacon walked up to the counter and waited for him to look up. When it was evident that he wasn't going to, Deacon spoke up.

"We were here earlier and talked to a guy named Levi. Is he around?"

Again, without looking up he said, "Nope. Left for the day."

"Do you know where he went?" Deacon was getting frustrated with the rudeness of the guy, who for all he knew he could have been a customer.

"Nope."

"When will he be back?"

"Maybe tomorrow, I'm not sure. He just said he had to go and left. Now is there anything else I can do for you?"

Deacon wanted to yank him out of the chair but instead just said, "Nope."

Nick was behind Deacon and had listened to the whole conversation. They looked around the shop as they headed for the door. Once they were outside, they walked around the back of the shop to see if Levi was out there. The back was full of empty boxes but there were no signs anyone had been there. The grass was overgrown and the area too full of trash to be used as a parking area. They walked back to the front and over to the truck.

"He's not here. Bevis in there said he left earlier and wasn't sure when he was coming back."

Nick laughed. "I thought Deacon was going to grab the guy and beat the heck out of him. He was really rude so I wouldn't have blamed him. I wasn't even in the conversation, and I wanted to tear into him. Good job keeping your cool, brother."

Carsyn could tell that Deacon was still annoyed with the guy but was trying to put the whole thing out of his mind. She knew that he was the least of their worries at the moment. They needed to find Levi and get some explanation as to why he was at the theatre. From what the man told Deacon they would have to wait until tomorrow for those answers.

"Another dead end, at least for now." Carsyn inhaled and exhaled before she spoke. "Where to now. It seems like we're going in circles like on a merry-go-round and random people keep jumping on and off. Now we have to look at Levi as a suspect. Where does it end?" Carsyn shuddered at the thought of where this could actually end up. She felt like he was hiding something, but she wasn't sure it was connected to her carjackers.

CHAPTER TWENTY-SEVEN

Time was passing quickly because it was already 6 days since she was carjacked, and she still didn't know who carjacked her or why they were still after her. After a day of hitting dead ends, Deacon suggested they go back to the rental and start fresh again tomorrow morning. She hated to give up, but she knew he was right, and they could all use another good night's sleep.

She took a long hot shower and tried to wash away the disappointment of the day. It wasn't that they hit dead end after dead end in locating her attackers that had her heart wrenched in pain, it was the yearning to see Cami.

The wound on her leg was healing nicely although it would take a while to completely heal. She touched her shoulder, and the pain reminded her that she had injured it when she fell to the ground. *Lord, I'm all beat up.* She finished her shower and called Deacon in for his turn. As they crossed paths, Deacon kissed the top of her head and told her how much he loved her. She responded that she loved him more and then left the bathroom in search of her bed. Usually it took a while for her to fall to sleep, but she felt very sleepy and hoped that tonight would be like the last and she'd fall out quickly.

Carsyn sat down on the edge of the bed and said a quick prayer before leaning back onto her pillow. *God's Will Be Done!* Those were the words Cami lived by. The thought of Cami floating around out there with no purpose made her feel anxious. *Surely, Cami was in heaven with mom and dad. She just can't remember when she crosses over to my side. That has to be it.* She was trying to soothe her mind with positive thoughts and eventually went off to sleep.

When she woke up she was back in the hospital. The room was dark and quiet, and the only sound she heard was the beeping of the machine. Deacon was sleeping in the same chair next to her bed. *How am I here again? Did something happen that I don't remember?* Carsyn thought hard hoping to dredge up what had happened to land her back in the hospital. Nothing came to her mind.

She closed her eyes and took a few deep breaths. *Do not panic. You are strong. You can handle this. Get a grip. You are strong and can weather any storm. You cannot be stopped! You are the storm!* She repeated those words over and over and after each time, she was calmer until finally she was completely in control of her emotions again.

The thought of the man behind the curtain surfaced and her eyes shot in that direction. The curtain wasn't moving but she wasn't convinced that he wasn't still there. She attempted to get up but the line from the machine was still hooked to her arm confining her to the bed. She stayed completely still pretending to be sleeping while she tried to devise a plan to deal with the situation. The last thing she heard was the sound of Deacon's voice calling out her name, but she couldn't respond.

Carsyn bolted upright in the bed and this time she was face to face with Deacon who was standing over her still in bed at the rental house.

"Where am I?" Her eyes were wild, and her breathing was fast and heavy. She was swinging her arms until one landed across Deacon's chest. He grabbed her hands and said her name.

This time in a whisper she said, "Where am I?"

"Carsyn look at me. You're safe, honey. We're at the rental house. Do you remember? We came here to hide out for a while. Carsyn can you hear me? You're safe." Deacon kept his voice low and calm.

"How is that possible. I was just back in the hospital. What happened? Did they find us?" Carsyn stood up quickly and assessed her body for new injuries. Her leg still appeared to be healing, at least no bleeding. And her shoulder still hurt but other than that, she was fine.

"I must've been dreaming, right? But it was so real. You were there sleeping in a chair like before and the room was dark and quiet. I could still hear that stupid machine beep."

"That had to be the quickest dream ever because you were awake just a minute ago when I walked into the room from the shower. I was just getting ready to get into bed and when I said your name to tell you good night, you freaked out."

"No, I had to be dreaming. I heard you calling my name, but I couldn't wake up. I couldn't answer you. I couldn't respond at all." The last few words came out as a whisper.

She watched as Deacon went to his side of the bed and got in dragging himself up against her. He wrapped his warm arms around her, pulled her into an embrace and made her feel safe. She could feel his love. She stayed there in his arms the rest of the night unable to go to sleep but instead focused on sweet memories of her childhood when both of her parents and Cami were still around, and her life was happy and full without a care in the world.

She remembered swinging on the big tire swing that hung from the big oak tree in their front yard. Her parents, Joseph and Amanda Carlin, lived on three acres and every day was a new adventure for the Carlin Girls. Cami would push her so high in the swing that she'd squeal as she reached the highest point right before her stomach dropped as she came back toward the ground.

Even though Cami was eight years older, she always found time to spend with Carsyn and she was always there to protect her. She was blessed to have amazing parents along with an amazing big sister. Her childhood was filled with love and laughter every day. *No wonder it took me so long to grow up.* There was always someone there to protect her, even when her parents were gone, Cami continued to protect her.

There were hard times, like scraped knees, bullies at school, disappointments, and the loss of their wonderful grandmother when she was fourteen but while the losses were hard, her families love, and support made them survivable.

Cami was married to a career military man who was often gone for months at a time on tours in other countries. She spent a lot of time at their parents' house when Brad was out of the country on tour, but after their mom died she focused most of her attention on their dad and her. Cami's husband was still working around the world but had stayed in touch with Carsyn whenever he could.

A rooster crowed announcing the arrival of yet another day without being any closer to getting answers. Carsyn didn't let that discourage her but instead let it fuel her need to take control of things and go out and find those dangerous men. In the back of her mind, nestled quietly next to the memories of the woman they found in the woods, was the thought that with each passing moment another woman could be in danger or worse already dead. *I will never give up on you.* She didn't know why her life was spared that day if not to help catch them before they could carjack someone else.

She was up and dressed before the rooster crowed a second time. She thought she was the only one up but when she walked into the kitchen, Avery was there sipping her coffee.

"That smells wonderful." Carsyn walked over, poured a cup and then sat down at the table. She glanced out the back door and noticed the yellow field of flowers and smiled.

Avery was pleased to see Carsyn calm. "It's good to see that smile again. Let's go sit outside on the porch. It's a bit muggy but the view is spectacular, and I know you love your yellow flowers. How are you doing this morning? Did you sleep well?"

Carsyn wanted to say, 'No! How could I sleep well when those men are still out their terrorizing other people' but instead shrugged her shoulders. She wanted to scream at the top of her lungs and smash something. She wanted to kick and scream and cry like a baby. She wanted someone to tell her everything would eventually go back to normal. She wanted her dead sister to come back and stay with her forever. But none of those things were going to happen and she learned a few years ago when Cami died that she had to 'adult up' and face things head on. She hadn't realized how much Cami shielded her and how well she looked after her until she was gone. Aside from the devastation of losing her sister, she had to learn how to be a grown up and face whatever the world threw at her by herself. And she had done that. She had learned to navigate through life, sinking at times, but always fighting to stay above water without her sister and she had finally found her way to the surface. Seeing Cami again had temporarily tossed her into a tailspin, but she woke up feeling strong and was ready to be the storm once again.

She heard activity in the kitchen again and waited to see who was up. Deacon walked out the door onto the patio and greeted them good morning. She smiled at the way his hair was always flipped up in the middle when he first woke. She knew they had to decide what to do next because both Deacon and Nick had to get back to work soon. They owned and operated a string of storage unit facilities across the area along with several rental properties. They were usually hands on every day but had sat back this past week. Both Carsyn and Avery work part time to handle the accounting part of the companies which allowed them to work from anywhere.

"I think we need to make some tough decisions here." Deacon stated as he found a chair next to his wife and sat down.

"I know. We have to get back to reality and back to work." Carsyn looked defeated. "I thought for sure that we would've found out something by now. Just think how awful it must be for people who lose loved ones and never know where they are or what happened to them. Can you imagine? I can't handle the fact that it's been 6 days, and we don't have a lead."

"That's not completely true. We know they drove a white van and you have a partial license plate number. We know they have a tattoo of a cross on their wrist and a pocketknife with the same cross on it. We also need to find Levi and see what his connection is to all of this." Deacon wanted to reassure his wife that they were not giving up. "Sweetheart, you've been through a lot and the things you were able to remember will help us in the end." He knew she wasn't only talking about the carjacking but also the need to find her sister.

Carsyn shrugged her shoulders and then smiled at her husband. "Thank you for being the optimistic one today. Have you heard from Detective Stevens?"

"Not yet. I do need to call him and get an update. What do you want to do about Levi? Should we tell him?" He knew Carsyn was apprehensive about the detective and wasn't sure what she wanted him to know.

"What do ya'll think we should do?" Carsyn looked at Deacon and Avery for guidance. "I don't know why I got the feeling we can't trust him but something's off with him. Maybe he's just lazy or maybe he's so busy with other cases but with the information we've given him, he should know something. Why can't they find the van? Oh, and when I walked up to him at the shop he was leaning over the dead body and slipped something into his pocket. Can we go back to the tattoo shop today and talk to Levi first? Then, we can tell the detective and let him handle it."

"Carsyn, we can take all the time we need to make sure you are safe but you're right, sooner or later we have to get on with our lives. Maybe you and Avery should consider going to the TAC Scrapbook Convention this weekend. It would be a great place to hide out for a few more days and Nick and I can continue to check out tattoo parlors in the area. Doesn't it start tomorrow? Ya'll already paid to go so why not just go." Deacon didn't want her out of his sight, but he knew that was unrealistic thinking and decided that maybe she'd be safer away from home.

Nick finally joined them on the patio and the four of them agreed to go back and visit Levi. Then, if that were a dead end, they would turn everything over to the Detective and she and Avery would go to TAC.

CHAPTER TWENTY-EIGHT

The night before, after going back to the tattoo parlor to look for Levi, who wasn't there again, they went to lunch at Gattuso's Restaurant, then called it a day. Deacon called Detective Stevens and gave him all the information they had and asked him to keep them posted. They also made another visit back to the Church looking for Cami but to no avail. Carsyn didn't want to go to the convention for four days without at least trying to find Cami one more time. The twist she felt in her stomach stayed with her for the remainder of the day and into the night.

First thing in the morning, Carsyn and Avery started to prepare for the TAC convention. The theme was always Pink Flamingos, and this year Social Butterflies was added. They usually decorated their tables according to the theme but with everything they had going on they'll have to depend on the other ladies to handle it this time. Her entire group always goes overboard with decorations so she felt confident their table would be well represented.

Deacon and Nick went home to gather Caryn and Avery's scrapbook materials and she thought how interesting it would be to see if they got the right items. Lucki-ly, both she and Avery had packed up what they were going to need well ahead of time. Deacon thought it was insane when he saw the amount of stuff they brought with them. He and Nick were going to drive them to the hotel in the rental truck, but they needed two vehicles just to fit everything. It had been a few days since they felt like they were being followed or had seen the white van, so Nick used his truck and Deacon used the rental. They took the long way around, stopping in the city for lunch before they headed to the hotel.

The convention was held in one of the larger rooms at the hotel, so once she and Avery were there, they didn't have to leave for four days. She just hoped that she would be able to relax and enjoy the festivities of the long week-end. She was still feeling paranoid and very suspicious of everyone around her. There were almost one hundred women attending the convention, but she knew most of them and wasn't worried about the rest. TAC sold out almost a year in advance so it wasn't like someone new could just sign up at the last minute.

As they approached the front of the hotel, Carsyn's heart began to pump faster. She clasped her hands togeth-er and noticed that they were sweating. She must have been excited to be there or maybe it was her nerves. She wasn't sure what the cause of the accelerated heart rate was, but decided that either way she was going to have fun. Once she was in and settled, she would relax and for-get about the total chaos her life had been the last week.

Deacon was unloading her stuff while she went to the front desk to check into her room. She and Avery shared a room every year and this year their friend Jackie was going to stay a few of the nights with them. The convention was local so many of the ladies went home at night. Carsyn always stayed because they always had the most fun late at night when they took a break from scrapbooking to line dance, play games and socialize.

She was next in line to check in. Her mind was hopping from what she was going to do first, to wondering what Detective Stevens was up to concerning her case, to what was Levi's connection, to where was Avery. She shook her head trying to get focused. *This should be a fun weekend.* The lady in front of her had finished checking in and it was now her turn.

She stepped up to the desk while looking down in her purse, fishing around for her driver's license and credit card, as the clerk asked if he could help her. The sound of his voice was alarmingly familiar and caused her to jolt and drop her purse. Avery came up behind her and helped retrieve her things. Carsyn inhaled and tried to remain calm. She stood up and stared at the desk clerk. She'd expected to calm down once she looked at him and realized that he didn't look familiar but that didn't happen. She was glad Avery recognized that something was wrong and stepped up to the desk to give their information for check in. Carsyn, unable to speak, stood there staring at the desk clerk trying to make a connection. She looked down at his wrist, but he was wearing a long sleeve shirt with a sweater.

She jerked her body around and headed to one of the couches in the lobby. While sitting there she kept her eyes on the clerk watching his every move. Not once did he look in her direction. She noticed he had a green jacket, and his hair was spiked bleached blonde. She studied his face trying to trigger her memory to figure out why he seemed so familiar. She stretched her neck hoping to get a glimpse of his arms from her position but only once, as he handed Avery the keys, they came into view but disappeared behind the desk quickly. She cupped her hands together, brought them up to her mouth and exhaled slowly. She was so deep in concentration that she didn't see Deacon walk into the hotel lobby until he approached Avery who pointed him in Carsyn's direction.

"Did something happen? Why do you look like you just saw a ghost? Carsyn, what happened?" Deacon left the luggage cart full of her scrapbook supplies in the middle of the floor and went to her side.

"I'm sorry. I'm okay. When I went to check in, the desk clerk's voice sounded familiar and then when I saw him my body just tensed up. I keep trying to figure out why I think I recognize him, but I keep drawing a blank. I think I'm just paranoid and high strung from everything that's happened. I'll be okay. He doesn't seem to recognize me or at least he hasn't looked up once since I walked away." Carsyn stood up and started to walk to the luggage cart. "Besides how would anyone know that I'd be here today and be able to get a job behind the desk that quick. That would be insane."

They were making their way from the lobby to the elevators when she felt someone's eyes on her back. She turned around just as the desk clerk bent down behind the desk. The elevator doors opened, and they got in and pressed two. She held her breath until the doors closed anxious that she was moving away from another unnerving situation. *Stop being so ridiculous.* Carsyn was trying to reason with herself because she didn't want her whole weekend to be haunted by the front desk clerk who was clearly uninterested in her. She reassured herself that once they got into the scrapbook room with the other women she'd calm down and forget all about the mysterious front desk clerk.

She had to convince Deacon that she was going to be okay and that he could leave. In spite of his uneasiness about leaving her, he agreed it was time to go. They all walked back to the elevators and went back down to the lobby where they left all of their scrapbook supplies. Deacon kissed her forehead and squeezed her tight before walking away from her.

"Are you ready?" Avery looked at Carsyn.

"Ready. I'm sorry that you have to push my stuff as well as your own into the room. I'm glad that for once I packed light."

When they entered the room Lori met her at the door and asked how she was doing. Then a few other ladies walked up trying to be supportive. Carsyn wasn't ready for all the questions but was grateful for their concern. She'd forgotten that everyone knew what had happened to her and understood that they were only asking out of concern. After a brief exchange, they all settled down and went on with whatever they were doing before she walked in. She was teary eyed but not because she was upset but because of the overwhelming love and support from not only her friends there but from other scrapbooking women she was only acquainted with. She felt loved and with the attention of almost one hundred women she felt safe.

She and Avery found their table and unloaded the luggage cart. Well Avery unloaded the cart while Carsyn sat down in her chair and rested her leg. She was instructed not to pick up anything heavy and to rest her leg when she could. Soon after they arrived, Linda and Peggy joined them. After the initial chit chat, they all settled in and started to share what they planned to work on. Carsyn smiled to herself and started to believe that maybe she would be able to relax and have a little fun.

CHAPTER TWENTY-NINE

By Saturday night, Carsyn was relaxed and had only thought about the carjackers every couple of hours instead of every few minutes and at every turn. She couldn't line dance, but she enjoyed watching and cheering her friends on. She considered getting up and joining in the second line but after grabbing her napkin, decided that would be pushing it so again she cheered everyone on from her chair. She also joined in the explosion of laughter when Lori came out wearing a pink flamingo suit and pranced around the floor. She loved those ladies.

Deacon had checked in almost every hour to make sure everything was going alright and to let her know the progress of their search for the cross tattoo. The last text she received said that they had checked out three other tattoo parlors but still no luck. They also went back to see if they could catch Levi, but he was still not there. She texted back asking if he had heard anything from Detective Stevens and his answer was short, "No."

The ladies finished line dancing and were back at the table. Carsyn was having a conversation with a woman she had just met, Lynn, about photography and other hobbies besides scrapbooking that they like to participate in. They hit it off right away especially when Lynn showed her a photo of a field of yellow flowers. Her immediate reaction was excitement.

"I love yellow flowers. This picture is beautiful."

"I'll send it to you if you'd like." Lynn was ready to share.

"That would be great. Thanks." Carsyn shared her phone number. Then the oddest feeling surged through her body. She watched as Lynn shared the photo then went on to talk to the other ladies about pictures. Carsyn quickly opened the picture and examined it for any familiar features. *Could this be a photo of the field by the church where I was left for dead? Or is it a photo of the side of the rental house I'm currently staying at?* As far as she could tell it was just a random picture of a field of yellow wildflowers but still she felt like she needed some fresh air.

"I'll be back." She grabbed her purse and slipped out of the conference room. There was a courtyard right outside the door, so she found her way out and into the hot humid night air.

She was angry with herself for finding suspicion in everything around her. *A picture of yellow flowers! Really!* While Carsyn had just met Lynn, she knew the group of ladies that Lynn was sitting with. She'd been friends with Roni for years and that was the same group of ladies that attended TAC ever year. Lynn was part of Roni's group.

She found a chair in the courtyard, sat down, and reopened the text message from Lynn. It really was a stunning picture. Visions of the yellow flowers she'd seen when she was left for dead reminded her of Cami. She wondered if she'd see her again. She knew she would. Deep down in her gut she knew her ordeal was not over yet and that if she was right and Cami appeared when Carsyn needed her, she'd see her again, soon.

Movement caught her attention from inside but when she looked up all she saw was the back of someone's jacket walking past the door. *Was that a green jacket*? The windows were tinted apparently to keep the heat out of the building during the day so she couldn't be sure what color she saw. It appeared dark but the tinted windows could've dulled a green jacket.

She looked around the courtyard to see if there were other exits and was relieved to learn there were several. She wasn't sure what to do. Her first instinct was to go in and follow the person, but she knew that wouldn't be smart to go all by herself. She was walking fairly good but if she had to run she'd be in trouble. She waited for a few minutes then just when she decided to go back in, Lynn walked out the door.

"Are you okay? Roni just told me what happened to you, and I was worried when you didn't come back." She sounded genuinely concerned.

"I'm good. Really. I just needed some air. In fact, I was just getting ready to come back in now." Carsyn got up and the two of them went back into the conference room. She really liked Lynn but for some reason still had reservations about her motive for showing her a picture of yellow flowers. Was that just coincidence or a perfectly timed reminder that she was being hunted and that nowhere was safe, and no one was above suspicion. *Listen to yourself. You sound like a crazy person.* She felt a little at odds with herself because she wasn't normally that paranoid and now the whole world around her was becoming a suspect.

Back at the table she forced herself to pull out some pictures of herself and Deacon from their trip to Maine. She laughed when the first picture of the pile was of a field of yellow flowers. Her shoulders lowered and her legs loosened, and she was beginning to feel more at ease. She was being ridiculous, and she knew it, so it was time to put all the conspiracy theories to rest and enjoy the little time left at the conference. She always hated Saturday night because it meant that it was almost over. The conference wasn't over until 2pm on Sunday but everyone always started to pack up and leave way before then.

Suddenly visions of Cami started popping in and out of her mind occupying her thoughts. They were so vivid that it distracted her from what she was doing. Cami seemed upset because she had the same stern look on her face in each vision. As time passed the frequency at which Cami's face appeared in her mind increased until she couldn't ignore it any longer. She told Avery she was headed to the bathroom and got up and excused herself.

The hotel was quiet except for the noise and laughter coming from the conference room behind her. Carsyn wondered how anyone in the hotel slept with all that noise then remembered the hotel was right by the airport and the rooms probably had soundproof windows and walls.

The bathroom was located down a long hall. Usually it was well lit but of course it appeared that the lights were out the farther she walked. Normally, she was okay with situations like that, but her thoughts were getting the best of her, and she found herself trembling. She let out a nervous giggle. *Girl, when all of this is over you're gonna have to see a heart doctor because your heart has stopped, warmed, split in two, pounded, raced, skipped a beat and all but quit working at every turn lately. Gee, when will it end?* Finally reaching the bathroom door, she pushed it open and walked in. *When did going to the bathroom become so dramatic?* Thank God the lights were on allowing her to leave the spooky darkness behind her.

She chose a stall in the middle. She was almost inclined to draw her legs up so that if someone entered they wouldn't know she was there. *Now you're just being silly.* She finished, flushed the toilet and sat there trying to gain the courage to walk back down the dark hallway when she heard the bathroom door swing open. Instinctively, she drew her legs up and wrapped her arms around them tightly as she listened.

Carsyn didn't know what to do. She knew it was probably just another lady from the convention but what if it wasn't? *Should I call out to them because that wouldn't be weird at all.* She was afraid that they would hear the sound of her heart losing control but she herself wasn't in control so there was nothing she could do about it but pray.

After what seemed like forever but was only a few minutes, the bathroom door swung open again and she heard her name.

"Carsyn, are you still in here?" Avery was looking for her.

Relief flooded over her like a cool wave of water, and she all but screamed "Yes!" She waited as Avery walked slowly past each stall until she reached the right one then she opened the door and pulled her into the stall closing and locking the door behind them.

"What are you…" Avery didn't get to finish her sentence because Carsyn's hand covered her mouth.

"Shh! Listen!" Carsyn was on top of the toilet, crouched down with her hand around Avery's mouth and her eyes wide open with fear.

"Someone else is in here with us." Carsyn whispered.

Avery looked up at her sister n law and tried to compose herself before the laugh that was welling up in her throat and threatening to escape would insult her. She peeled Carsyn's fingers away from her mouth one at a time. "Carsyn, this is a public bathroom. Of course there could be other people in here. What is wrong with you!"

"I'm telling you Avery, someone else is in here and has been for a while. What if they found us? What if the green jacket guy from the front desk is involved?" Carsyn saw how Avery was looking at her and knew she thought her behavior seemed extreme, but she didn't care. She had to trust her gut even though she didn't know what her gut was telling her.

Avery did think Carsyn was mentally out of control but continued to whisper just to appease her. "Please get down before you fall. Since when does staying a while in a stall mean you are up to no good? Girl, listen to your-self."

The sound of a single footstep on the tile floor resonat-ed throughout the bathroom followed by silence. Carsyn and Avery both froze. After about a minute, the sound of another footstep touched their ears. Avery put her foot on the toilet and straddled Carsyn, who was now sitting down with her legs pulled to her chest. They couldn't tell how far or close the footsteps were.

Carsyn cranked her neck back slowly to look up at Avery who was crouched down above her. If she weren't so terrified she would be laughing uncontrollably at their current predicament but when she saw the terror in Avery's eyes her own fear intensified. All they could do was listen and wait.

She watched Avery dig around in her purse, quietly, looking for something. She removed her hand without making any noise and showed Carsyn the canister of mace she was holding. That was no match for a gun but at least it was something. Her leg was starting to ache from being stretched into that position, but she couldn't put it down. She looked up again and managed a faint smile when she and Avery's eyes connected. Avery returned the same small smile and hoped someone else would enter the bathroom soon.

Instead, a flutter of footsteps raced across the floor of the extremely long bathroom and stopped right in front of the stall they were in. They closed their eyes and held their breath wishing they were invisible.

CHAPTER THIRTY

Carsyn woke up back in the hospital. She looked around the room and like before it was dark and quiet except for the beeping of the machine. Deacon was sleeping in the chair next to the bed. No way! Where am I? I wasn't sleeping so how did I wake up here again? Carsyn was confused and scared because the last thing she remembered was being in that bathroom stall with Avery and someone was approaching them. Oh my God Avery! Where are you? Carsyn was beside herself not knowing what was happening to her and not knowing if Avery was okay.

Again, just like the last time, her mind went to the man behind the curtain and her eyes shot to that direction. Although her heart was acting like she was running a race, her breathing was shallow. Short, quiet breaths. I must be losing my mind. Maybe I've lost too much blood and I have brain damage. The doctor had said if I hadn't gotten to the hospital when I did I would've died. Maybe that's it that I was so close to being dead that I can't recover. She closed her eyes and thought about giving into the fatigue that had quickly taken over.

She waited to fall to sleep or pass out or whatever was going to happen, but nothing ever did. The anxiety of everything that had recently happened was still there and she still was fearful of the man behind the curtain. Did she wake up before the man was behind the curtain or after he left the room? She strained her eyes to see if there was anything on the floor, like a pocketknife or men's shoes, but it was too far away to see clearly.

She thought of Cami and wished she were there. Hello. Cami, I need you. I thought you were supposed to come when I was in trouble. Carsyn thought back to the visions of Cami that flooded her mind and sent her to the bathroom. Was that a warning that something was going to happen? She just hoped that if Avery were still in danger, Cami would be there to help.

Deacon was stirring in his chair, but he didn't wake up. She thought about waking him but what was she going to say? He already must have thought that she was losing her mind because of the last episode when she didn't know where she was or how she'd gotten there.

He was amazing though. Carsyn adoringly watched her husband sleep and recounted all the ways he'd been there for her. She'd hoped that one day she could do the same for him and prayed that he'd stick around long enough for her to show that to him. She knew he wasn't going anywhere because he was the most kind and patient man she'd ever met, complete opposite of her in the patience department. Having acknowledged how impatient she was, she decided that she could have a little patience for once and let him sleep.

She couldn't tell if she was dreaming or if in reality she was in the hospital because it seemed she was slipping back and forth between the two places often. The memory of the men staring at her in the parking lot before the carjacking gave her shivers. She should have paid more attention to them and alerted someone in the store. Even the man that plowed into her shoulder could've possibly walked her out to her car. The horrible sequence of events leading up to the carjacking came one after the other and she was ready to scream when she heard Avery whispering her name and nudging her in her back.

CHAPTER THIRTY-ONE

She opened her eyes and found herself looking at the back of a bathroom stall door. She swayed to the side losing her balance and almost toppled off of the toilet. She was back in the bathroom with Avery and the intense fear she'd felt was still with her.

There was a shadow of someone standing completely still right outside the stall they were in. They watched in horror waiting for whoever it was to try and open the door. She leaned to the right to peer through the crack in the door and let out a bloodcurdling scream that she was sure reached the top floor of the hotel even penetrating the soundproof walls.

There was an eye peeking in at them through the crack and right before Avery pressed the button on the mace, Peggy screamed out, "What are ya'll doing! I know ya'll are up to something no good."

It took a minute for the voice to register then another minute for Carsyn and Avery to get down from the top of the toilet without hurting one another.

Still slightly apprehensive, she opened the door slowly and then stared at Peggy who was standing there with a bigger grin than she should have had.

"Are you kidding me? You scared us half to death." Carsyn walked out of the stall with Avery in tow.

"Golly, Peggy! What did you think we were doing in there?" Avery's words were hard to understand because she had started to laugh before she finished her sentence.

Carsyn tried to stifle her laugh but realized that was impossible and just let loose. The three of them were laughing uncontrollably to the point of hysteria and continued each time one of them attempted to speak. Eventually, one by one, they ran into the stall so that they wouldn't pee on themselves.

They were finally settled down and ready to go back to the convention when the door flew open, and Liz and Linda rushed in to see if they were okay.

"We heard a scream and came running. What are ya'll doing in here?" Liz was waiting for an answer but all she got were giggles then bursts of laughter that was infectious enough to pull her and Linda in.

Their laughter continued the rest of the night and was a pleasant distraction from all the negative energy that had surrounded her lately. It was times like these when she missed Cami most of all. Before she passed on, Cami wanted to do scrapbooking, but Carsyn thought it would be boring and never wanted to try it. Her sister would be right by her side having fun along with the rest of the women. She pushed the thought away and tidied up her table space.

Carsyn and Avery decided to call it a night and headed to the elevators. It was past Avery's bedtime and she had been a trooper staying up until the end every other night. Walking down the hall that led to the elevators provided her with a perfect view of the front desk. Green jacket guy wasn't there but instead an older woman was standing behind the desk. She wondered if he would be there again tomorrow. She decided to ask the new desk clerk about him and all she said was that he'd gone to lunch and never returned. Carsyn thought that was odd but when she further questioned the clerk she informed her that they had a high turnover, and it wasn't unusual for someone to just up and quit. Carsyn was feeling too good, so she decided to store that information to think about tomorrow.

Back in their room Avery got in the shower first. Carsyn called Deacon one final time that day.

"Hey, did I wake you?" She thought he sounded like he was sleeping.

"No, I was just watching a movie. How are you doing? Are you having fun?"

"I'm good. We had a lot of fun. I'll tell you later how Peggy scared the life out of me and Avery. It's funny looking back now but it wasn't at the time. Did you hear anything from Detective Stevens yet?" Carsyn was hopeful.

"Yeah. He called earlier. The tattoo recognition thing came up empty. Now he's thinking that maybe they got the tattoos in another country which validates his theory that they were probably illegal immigrants. He strongly believes that they are part of a human trafficking gang that has infiltrated the New Orleans area. He also said that they got a positive ID from the man they shot at the shop. He was known to be part of a gang that was involved in armed robberies and drug trafficking but no known association with carjacking that they know of. He did say that the tattoo was fairly new, and he thinks he recently graduated to carjacking and maybe even human trafficking. They usually go where the money leads. Oh and they have a lead on the man that broke into our house. They're looking for him now."

"Deacon why didn't you call me? That's a lot of information." She was annoyed that he waited to tell her this information.

"Hey, and what could you have done with any of it? Nothing. I didn't want to ruin your fun and had hoped that you were able to put it out of your mind for a little while. I decided it would be better to tell you tonight when you called me. I'm sorry if I upset you. Detective Stevens did say that the guy doesn't have a home address, but he has a few leads on him so they're hoping to catch up with him soon. He did say don't be disappointed if it takes a while because he knows they're looking for him and it won't be easy to find him."

"I guess that's good news. At least they have a name and possibly known areas that he frequents, right?" Carsyn wasn't sure how she felt about all the new information. Human trafficking. Wow that's scary. She shuddered at the thought that she was in the hands of human traffickers. But why would they let her go? Something was not adding up, but she didn't express her concerns to Deacon because he sounded optimistic, and she didn't want to bring him down.

They spoke on the phone for bit longer then Carsyn took her turn to shower. Jackie had made it up to the room by the time she was done, and they stayed up chatting for a while. Again they got a good laugh about Peggy scaring them in the bathroom but when they turned out the lights, Carsyn reexamined everything Deacon told her earlier and prayed that they would find her attackers soon.

CHAPTER THIRTY-TWO

Sunday always came so quickly when they were at the convention. On the first day, they'd set up and attempt to work on something, but it was usually the next day before their creativity would start to flow. Once that happened, they worked on pages trying to get as much done as possible because unlike a lot of the women there, Carsyn and Avery didn't scrapbook much at home. They planned to but life always got in the way.

They were all downstairs in the conference room packing up their stuff, slowly, not wanting the event to end. Carsyn loaded up her cart then decided to go up to the room one last time to make sure she didn't forget anything. Oddly, she hadn't felt that good since she was carjacked. She felt optimistic and hopeful. As much as she didn't want the convention to end, she was just as anxious to get home and go look for Cami.

She found herself humming her song in the elevator and as she walked along the hallway to her room she started to quietly sing it. She felt happy. She felt normal again. Her room was almost the last one in an extremely long hallway. She heard the elevator beep but didn't really pay attention to it until she heard a low whistle. She paused for a moment and then brushed it off and kept walking and singing. Again she heard the faint whistling and this time it sounded like her song.

Panic stricken, the words that she was singing were caught in her throat and she froze in place. She was afraid to turn around and feeling like her legs were going to fail her, she was left standing in the middle of the hallway. *Maybe it's Peggy. I'm going to kill her!* Instinct told her that it wasn't Peggy and that she needed to get to her room fast. She managed to do a half turn but didn't see anyone in the hallway. The low whistling continued reaching every nerve in her body. She started to shake uncontrollably but managed to force her feet to move. The closer she got to the room the closer the whistling sounded.

Luckily, she had her key card in her hand ready to open the door. *How could I be so careless to let my guard down! I knew better to think I was safe. They came looking for me with blazing guns so why would they stop now?* Her singing switched to talking to herself and beating herself up for getting in that situation. She was scared but at the same time she was angry with herself for not paying attention to her surroundings. She reached for her cellphone and dropped it to the floor.

Her hand was trembling as she tried to hold the key card against the locked door. It slipped out of her hands as well, and she watched as it fell to the ground. Her eyes widened as the severity of the situation took hold. *Hurry!*

Hurry! Hurry! She bent down to retrieve the card and was afraid to look back to see how close he was. She assumed it was a man, but she wasn't sure because she never did see him only heard the whistle that was getting closer and closer.

Finally, after what seemed like forever, the green light lit up and she pushed open the door. She turned to look before she stepped in and was stunned by who she saw coming toward her.

"It's you?" Carsyn didn't wait for a response but instead rushed through the door and slammed it behind her. *What do I do now?* She reached for her cell phone but realized she hadn't picked it up and had left it outside the door. *You're kidding me. How did I do that?* She ran to the window and saw Peggy and Linda just below her walking to their cars. She frantically banged on the window to get their attention, but they didn't look up. *No, no, no! Look up! PEGGY! LINDA! HELP! Anybody please help me!* She ran to the dresser and grabbed a glass to try and bang on the window. She pounded and pounded but the only sound was a dull noise inside the room. I need to break the window. She ran and grabbed a towel to wrap around her hand and when she reached the bathroom, the door handle to her room was jiggling. *Hurry!* She grabbed the towel and ran back to the window.

With her hand wrapped in the towel she picked up the glass and started to hit the window repeatedly while she kept shouting for help. The glass wouldn't break, and she was out of time. The door to the room opened and she had nowhere to hide. One last attempt to break the glass with a chair that was nearby failed and forced her to switch gears.

In her state of panic, it never occurred to her to use the telephone on the nightstand to call for help. He was in the room and still whistling her song as he walked slowly toward her. She backed up to the window and as he got closer she threw the chair at him hoping to knock him down. She jumped on to the bed toward the telephone. He watched her eyes as they settled on the phone, and he knew what she was thinking. She grabbed the receiver and hit nine for the front desk, but he was on top of her before anyone picked up and ripped the cord from the wall. For a moment she thought he was going to strangle her with the cord, but he threw it aside and backed away from her.

"What do you want?" She started tossing pillows at him. "Leave me alone! My friends are coming soon. They were supposed to be right behind me."

He just glared at her not saying a word until his cell phone rang so he pressed the answer button and just listened. "Got it." He ended the call and just stood there.

"Trust me, nobody's coming to your rescue."

Carsyn's heart completely stopped beating. *What did that mean? Did he do something to Avery or the others?* She knew she had to stay calm. *But why does he look so calm? What is he waiting for? Why didn't he kill me yet?* A lightbulb went off in her head like the cartoon characters when a thought comes to them. *He's not here to kill me. He wants something from me, but what could that be?* She was still terrified but a little relieved that maybe she was right, and he wanted her alive.

"What do you want from me? Please tell me what you want." Carsyn softened her tone and hoped to appeal to his sensitive side if he had one.

He didn't, because his gaze grew dark, and he grabbed her by the arm. "We can do this the easy way or the hard way."

Carsyn yanked her arm hard, kicked him and pushed him backwards.

"Why would I make it easy on you?" She was shouting at him as he approached her again.

"I didn't mean easy on me sweetheart, I meant easier on you." He grabbed her again. This time he covered her mouth and nose with a rag until within seconds she went limp and everything around her was fading to black.

"That smell" Carsyn's legs gave way and she fell into his arms.

CHAPTER THIRTY-THREE

Carsyn's eyes cracked open slowly. Her head was pounding, and her vision was blurred. There were small streams of light coming in from different places in the room. *Am I still in the hotel room?* She tried to focus and adjust her eyes to the low light and answered her own question when she saw bars on a small window. She quickly pulled her arms to her chest and was relieved that she wasn't tied up or shackled to the bed. At that thought she swung her legs up to make sure they were free as well. *How did I get here?* She tried to stand up but felt off balance, so she sat on side of the bed instead.

She took a quick glance around the room and determined that she was alone. Her shoulders slumped and she relaxed a little as she tried to figure out what to do next. There were a few other windows, but they had bars on them as well, making it clear she wasn't getting out by way of window. A mouse ran across the floor, and she had to slap her hand over her mouth to stifle her scream. Even though she was alone inside, she wasn't sure that someone wasn't close by, and she didn't want anyone to know she had regained consciousness. Not yet. She needed time to figure out where she was and what her next move should be.

She started to whisper. *Cami! I need you Cami. Where are you?* She smiled a bittersweet smile because she knew that she was in trouble, but that usually meant Cami was coming and that made her happy.

She started to feel back to normal, so she stood up and walked to the door. Disappointedly, when she reached the door she saw that it was just like that big door at the shop that Deacon said was reinforced steel and almost impossible to break into. In her case, it was impossible to break out.

She looked around and by the looks of the area she was in some sort of trailer. The windows were high, so she pushed a chair against the wall to look out. In the distance, she saw railroad tracks and a lot of grass, water and trees and that was it. She drug the chair over to the other side of the trailer and looked out that window to see much of the same - grass, water and trees. Before she stepped down from the chair she thought she saw movement farther in the distance. *A highway?* That could be the top of cars moving on a highway, but she wasn't sure. She refocused her vision and soon saw movement again. *An eighteen wheeler! Yes that's a highway.* Carsyn tried to find some sort of landmark that would tell her what highway, but there wasn't one, not one that she could see from that window anyway.

She had no idea how long she was unconscious or how far away from the hotel he took her. The hotel was on Airline Highway by the New Orleans airport in Kenner. The closest water to that area was Lake Pontchartrain but that was several miles away. From the hotel, Airline Highway led to the city of New Orleans in one direction and Baton Rouge in the other direction. Carsyn's eyes widened when she recalled that Airline also went to Baton Rouge because she was reminded that the Bonnet Carre Spillway wasn't far from the hotel and there were railroad tracks that ran parallel to Airline. *This might be the Bonnet Carre Spillway!* She got off the chair and tried to remember everything she knew about the spillway.

She used to go crawfishing there when she was young. There was a boat launch and a small campsite area. She jumped back up on the chair to see if any of that was visible, but it wasn't. She also remembered seeing four wheeler and motorcycle trails. Every time she traveled that way she saw a lot of activity on those trails. She strained to listen, but she didn't hear any motorized vehicles at all. In fact it was completely quiet except for the low hum of the air conditioner. Her head shifted around the room looking for the unit. She stopped looking when she saw the thermostat on the wall next to the door. *Shoot! Central Air. No window unit!* She needed to find a way out of there fast.

Carsyn wondered why Cami hadn't appeared yet. She was definitely in trouble and needed help. *Am I too far away from her?* She was afraid that she might be on her own and that was not something for which she was ready. She walked back to the bed and sat on the edge. She was tired, probably the results of the chloroform, and needed time to think.

She climbed back onto the chair and looked out of the window opposite the highway and noticed the tops of some round buildings way off in the distance. There were plenty of chemical plants on and around Arline Highway in that area and she was sure that was what she was seeing. After that revelation she was confident that she was somewhere in the spillway.

The last thing she remembered was going back to the room to get ready for check out on Sunday. That's when he followed her and eventually got into the room and sedated her. She wondered how he got into the room without a key. The green jacket guy came to mind, and she wondered if he had anything to do with her kidnapping. *Kidnapping, really. First carjacked and now kidnapped. This can't be happening.* She shut her eyes and hoped that when she opened them again it would all have been a dream.

Carsyn clinched her jaw and her face turned red as she shook her head in disappointment. She wanted to scream out in anger when she opened her eyes to the same room as before, but she knew she couldn't. The air condition fan had shut off and the only noise in the trailer was the air entering her nose as she inhaled slowly attempting to calm herself down. She was tired and scared and didn't want to face this anymore. She felt like a spoiled child that wanted someone to fix things for her and if she didn't get her way she was going to kick and scream, except there wasn't anyone there to help or to care if she kicked and screamed.

Carsyn slowly walked back to the bed and reluctantly sat down. Her head rested in her hands while she sat and quietly sobbed. Eventually she laid back and gave in to the feeling of defeat. Her head throbbed and her leg was beginning to ache. The Tylenol she'd last taken had since worn off allowing the pain from being shot to return. She didn't have much time to wallow in her pain and sorrow before the sound of someone turning the handle of the door brought her back to reality.

Carsyn scooted to the other side of the bed and silently slid off to the floor. She knew there was nowhere to hide but felt a little comfort with the bed between her and the door and the person on the other side of it. She waited as the door gradually opened and he walked into the trailer.

She didn't move but instead waited to see what he was going to do next. She was not going to be cooperative in any way, so he had better be ready for a fight.

He walked into her view with his hands raised and his eyes immediately rested on hers.

"I'm not here to hurt you." He stopped a few steps inside the door.

She didn't say anything because his words meant nothing to her. He kidnapped her and was keeping her hostage in a trailer in the middle of nowhere and he expected her to trust him.

"I swear, I won't hurt you. I brought you some pain medicine and some Tylenol for your leg. I brought supplies." He continued walking to the table and set the bag down.

The word supplies caught her attention. That means that he intended to keep her there for a while. She felt like she was going to throw up but instead was reminded that she hadn't eaten in a while. He brought food and medicine, but she couldn't eat any of it, how could she? It could all be poisoned. Her mind was working overtime as she considered what he was saying. *Why would he poison me now? He could've already killed me if he wanted me dead. So he wants me to be alive, but why? What does he want from me?* Carsyn stayed silent and waited for him to make the first move.

Instead of going after her he turned and walked back toward the door. Panic raged through her body. She was scared to be left there all alone again even though she thought that he was a threat. She wanted more time to think things over. She needed more time, but he was leaving, and her time had run out.

"Wait!"

He stopped at the door and listened to her plea.

"What do you want from me? Why am I here?" She waited for answers.

She could tell he was conflicted and hoped that he would tell her what she needed to know but instead Levi opened the door and walked out, locking it behind him.

The word "no" slipped from her lips at the sound of the lock clicking into place.

CHAPTER THIRTY-FOUR

Carsyn jolted awake to find that she was on the floor next to the bed. Light was shining through the windows offering brightness to the dark room. She was momentarily dazed as she stretched out her stiff body and canvassed the room. The memory of Levi walking out the door rushed into her mind, but she was too weak to respond. Instead, she pulled herself up and onto the bed and took a moment to think.

She glanced at the bag still sitting in the same spot he'd put it and just stared. He'd said that he had brought her medicine and supplies which must include food. She debated if eating his food was a good idea and decided that she had no choice if she hoped to find a way out of there. She would need her strength and besides, her leg was throbbing even more than before.

She walked over to the table and grabbed the Tylenol. She'd noticed earlier there was bottled water in the fridge, so she took one out and swallowed three Tylenols. There were chips and cookies in the bag as well but before she ate she wanted to see if she could determine what time of the day it was. She was unconscious when she had arrived there and wasn't even sure what day it was.

Carsyn climbed on top of the chair again and looked out the window. The sky was light to her right which would be east. The grass looked damp like it was covered in morning dew. *Morning time. It's early morning.* Carsyn's eyes moved from east to west looking for any signs of life but all she saw was the occasional car far off in the distance.

The image of the food in the bag was nagging at her and she knew sooner or later she'd have to eat something, so she gave in and grabbed an unopen bag of chips. She was hungrier than she realized and gobbled down the whole bag before she knew it then reached for some water. She was so busy guzzling the water that she didn't hear the door open behind her until she heard his voice.

"Oh my God!" Carsyn swung around terrified, dropped her water bottle and was ready to defend herself.

"Hang on Bruce Lee. Like I told you before, I'm not here to hurt you. Relax, please." Levi stayed put by the door.

"Really? Relax. Would you if you were kidnapped and held hostage in a trailer? Well, would ya?" Carsyn felt braver and even placed her hands on her hips as she spoke.

Levi walked across the room and sat down on a chair away from her. "Wow! Why are you so difficult? I didn't think you would be so much trouble."

She perked up. "What do you want? Why did you kidnap me and why am I a hostage?"

"First off, you're not a hostage. I am here to help you. Some bad people are after you, and I am here to protect you so let me do my job."

"Really this is how you protect someone by locking them in a trailer in the spillway?"

"What did you say? How did you know that we're in the spillway?" Levi looked surprised.

"Does that really matter? I want to know what it is that you want from me."

Levi lowered his eyes and answered her. "I can't tell you that." He looked up again and hoped that she would listen to him. "All I can tell you is that some dangerous people are looking for you and I am the only thing standing between you and them. You'll just have to trust me."

Carsyn chuckled at his suggestion to trust him. He must be a psychopath because no one in their right mind would expect their kidnapped victim to trust them.

"This has to do with the men that carjacked me and left me for dead, right? What are they, human traffickers who are afraid that I can identify them? I knew when I saw you at the tattoo parlor that there was something suspicious about you. No tattoos was a dead giveaway."

"Those men are the least of your problems. This is bigger than those small town hoodlums, believe me. They are dangerous and need to be stopped but they were hired to find and retrieve something valuable by some people that are far worse and will stop at nothing to get what they want, even murder." He stopped talking and looked down at her leg.

Self-consciously she touched her leg before speaking. She wondered what could be more dangerous than human trafficking. Her gut told her that he wasn't there to hurt her, but she still didn't trust he was there to protect her either. "Exactly what is it that they want?"

Again he averted his eyes when she answered. "I can't tell you that. I said too much already. You just need to trust me. It's for your own good." He reached into his pocket and when he pulled out his hand a cell phone fell to the ground.

"My phone. You have my phone. What did you do to Avery?"

"What?"

"What did you do to Avery? In the hotel room you said that no one was coming to my rescue. What did you do to her?" Carsyn braced herself for the answer.

"Avery's fine. Everyone's fine for now. These men are looking for you and they know that I have you. That should stop them from going after your family."

She backed down. "I don't understand. Why would they go after my family? I don't have anything of value so what do they want?"

The more she spoke, the more he looked agitated. "I told you that I can't tell you so enough with the questions. We have to get out of here."

"I'm not going anywhere with you. I don't believe you. How do I know that you didn't hurt Avery back at the hotel?"

Levi was tired and just wanted her to listen to him. He reached back into his pocket and fished out a cell phone. Her cell phone. She lunged forward to grab it, but he backed up before she could.

"Listen, you have the ring app on your phone right?"

She reached out for the phone again, but he pulled it back. "Yes, I have ring. Why?"

He raised up his hand motioning for her to stay put. He turned on the phone and waited. "What's your password?"

She looked at him like he was nuts.

"Look, do you want proof that Avery's alright or not?"

She still didn't want to give him her password, so he held the phone out for her to put her password in. Once it opened he scrolled through and found the ring app. He searched the history and found where Deacon, Avery and Nick entered the back door of her house late yesterday afternoon. He quickly turned off the phone again and shoved it into his pocket.

"Now, can we please talk seriously. We need to move soon."

Something tapped the side of the trailer. Levi grabbed her and threw her to the floor just as the barrage of bullets sprayed the trailer. He crawled over to the other side of the bed and pushed it over, exposing a hatch under a rug. He pulled open the hatch and then pulled her to it. Her hands had covered her ears and she'd balled up like a baby trying to protect herself.

"Go! Go! Go!" After she lowered herself down he followed and then led her out the back. They crawled through the marsh as the bullets continued to fly.

At one point, Carsyn froze and laid still in the marsh. She'd started to cry and was afraid for her life. She felt a nudge and looked up to see Cami standing over her.

"Cami. You came!"

"Keep moving little sister. Keep moving." Cami's voice sounded urgent.

"I can't! I'm so tired. Why does this keep happening? When will this end? I just want to go home."

She looked ahead to Levi and noticed that he'd stopped as well. She wondered what role he played in everything. Why didn't he just leave her?

"Come on Carsyn, move. You don't have that much further to go. Move!"

"Stop yelling at me!"

Levi looked confused. "I'm not yelling at you! But you have to come on. Once they realize that we're not in the trailer they're going to come looking for us. Give me your hand."

She looked up at Cami who was shaking her head yes. "Do it Carsyn! He's your only hope right now."

She reached out her hand and grabbed onto his and together they crawled away from the sounds of gunfire.

CHAPTER THIRTY-FIVE

The marsh was difficult and scary to wade through. Just when she thought they had reached hard ground they found themselves deeper in the marsh. The gunfire continued long after they'd escaped the trailer but eventually stopped. Just as Levi suspected, voices and the sound of people walking in their direction radiated through the air and confirmed that they were being pursued. She shuddered to think what else was in that marsh with her. Cami stayed with her but kept quiet only pushing her when she needed pushing.

When the men following them got too close, Cami went in a different direction to distract them. That gave Carsyn and Levi a chance to get farther away and hopefully to safety.

"Do you have a plan?" Carsyn whispered to Levi hoping that he did.

"Just keep moving. We're almost there."

"Almost where? Where are we going?" She was exhausted and knew she couldn't make it much further.

They heard more gunfire in the opposite direction. Levi stood up and without warning scooped Carsyn up into his arms and pushed forward. In the distance she could see the railroad tracks and a vehicle parked next to them. At first glance the truck looked old and useless but as they got closer she could see that it was in decent shape, at least decent enough to get them out of there.

"Is that your truck?" She prayed that it was.

"Please stop talking."

Angered by his rudeness, she wanted to scream at him but knew that would be a bad idea. She just had to put up with him until she could get away. She was afraid that the men after them were going to eventually go after her family and she needed to warn them. If he were really trying to help her why wouldn't he just get her to the police station or at least let her call Deacon? Did he think that he could protect her better than the police?

They finally reached the truck, and he lowered her down to the seat of the passenger side. He went to the driver's side and opened the door but instead of getting in and starting the truck, he pushed it forward. She looked over her shoulder and was thankful that they were still alone. She wondered where Cami was.

After what seemed like forever, Levi hopped in the truck, turned the ignition and slowly drove down the shell road eventually turning onto Airline Highway. His shoulders slacked and she saw relief spread across his face. She wanted to ask where they were going but she knew he wasn't going to tell her. She just made mental notes of her surroundings and prayed that he was being truthful and could be trusted.

Her eyes were heavy with exhaustion and her body ached. They continued to drive in silence and before long she fell asleep. When she woke they were still in the truck, but they weren't moving. She rubbed her eyes and when she opened them she was back in the hospital. She straightened up and frantically rubbed her eyes again and found herself back in the truck. She felt like she was losing her mind. Levi noticed her erratic behavior and asked if she was alright.

The blank look on her face contradicted the nod yes that she'd offered as an answer. She was grateful that he didn't push the issue because she didn't have an explanation to give him. She looked down at her leg looking for blood as a reason for her confusion. She blamed blood loss the last time that happened, but she wasn't bleeding anymore. In fact, her leg was healing up nicely considering the trauma she had endured time and time again.

The blank look shifted to confusion because she didn't know what was happening to her. She was jumping from one reality to another or rather from reality to delusion and back again. *How do I know what's real and what's not?* She pinched her arm hoping to wake up from a bad dream, but nothing happened, she was still in the truck with Levi staring at her.

She thought she saw a glimmer of sympathy in his eyes but that went away just as quickly as it had appeared. At least he hadn't hurt her yet and he did get her away from the men with the guns. But maybe those men were after him not her. Her life was in a tailspin, and she didn't know how to stop it.

They were sitting silent until Carsyn looked around, took note of her surroundings and realized where she was.

Her head swung around to him. "We're in Crown Point. Why are we in Crown Point? Am I going home? Bring me home!"

"This is where those idiots that carjacked you were dumping the bodies of victims that didn't make it." He watched as the horror made its way across her face. He knew that she had been dumped there as well and the effect it would have on her. "They're preoccupied right now looking for you so I felt like this would be a good place to hide out until we figured out what to do." He looked away then continued. "I know this brings up painful memories, but I thought it was the right move at this point."

She didn't know what to make of him. That was the second time she noticed a look of sympathy toward her on his face. She settled down and remained silent again. What was upsetting was the fact that she was so close to home and her family, yet she couldn't get to them. She wondered what he'd do if she jumped out of the truck and ran away. She looked down at her leg and it was a reminder that she wouldn't get far. Maybe she could persuade him to, at the very least, let her call Deacon. But, what if he were right and that would put Deacon and her family in danger? She made the decision to stay put for the moment and see if she could get him to tell her what exactly was going on.

She started talking in a low, calm voice and hoped that he would feel sorry for her. "I'm fine. You're right, they did leave me here to die but this is not the first time that I came back since the attack. The moment I was out of the hospital, I raced over here to..." She stopped abruptly. She was about to say, 'find Cami my sister who passed on several years ago' but thought better of it. He would think she was crazy for sure. "We came back here right after because I wanted to face the trauma head on. In fact, we found one of their victims still alive over there in that wooded area. That poor woman was all alone and almost dead." She noticed Levi's face twitch as she spoke about another woman left for dead. "I still don't understand why they dumped us if they are part of a human trafficking gang? Did something go wrong? I thought that it was because I could identify them but you say that's not why they're after me so what is it?"

Levi remained silent as usual.

"Did you know that they came back and followed me and Avery trying to run us off the road? What makes you think that they won't come back again? And what is your part in all of this? Are you working for the bad guys or the good guys? You said you were here to protect me, and your actions have proven that to be true so far, so which is it? Good or bad?" She expected him to get angry but instead he looked sad and uncomfortable.

He ran his hand over his head and just sighed.

"Please, I need to know."

The sadness was replaced with anger and he all but shouted at her. "I told you it's too dangerous." He leaned forward and grabbed her arm to make sure he had her full attention. "Listen Love. These men that are after you are some of the most dangerous men in the world and all we can hope for is to find what they want before they get to you. You need to help me. Did you find anything out of the ordinary when you woke up on the ground or at the hospital? It would be something really small like a flash drive. Apparently they think you have it, and they will not stop until they get it back. Think Carsyn! Please."

She was rattled. She answered in an unsteady voice. "No. I don't have what they want."

By the look on his face she knew what he was thinking. He'd hoped that she had what they wanted, and he could get it back to them because if they find her and she doesn't have it, well that would not end well. They wouldn't believe her of course and she shuddered at that thought. *Okay so he is trying to help me, but why? If these men are so dangerous why would he risk his life for me?* Why couldn't it have just been an ordinary carjacking that went wrong then it would all be over but instead she was running for her life.

CHAPTER THIRTY-SIX

Once Levi was convinced that she understood the severity of their situation he pulled the truck behind the church to keep out of sight. He got out of the truck and told her she could too if she wanted to. She opened the door and winced when she stepped down.

Levi ran to her side to help her. "Hang on." He leaned into the passenger side and opened the glove box to retrieve a bottle of Tylenol. "There's a bottle of water on the back seat."

"Thanks. Oh my God!" When she glanced past him toward the wooded area a horrible thought crossed her mind. "What if they dumped someone else in there. We gotta go check."

Levi grabbed her wrist and stopped her. She stood there waiting for him to tell her why that wasn't a good idea but instead he opened the back door and got a bottle of water for her.

"Take the Tylenol, please. You need to be ready for anything and if you're in pain..." He didn't finish his sentence. He waited for her to swallow the pills then started walking toward the woods. "Are you coming?"

A slight smile surfaced as she quickly fell in step behind him. He reminded her of an older brother always ready to scold her but in the end giving in to what she wanted to do. She'd always wanted a brother, not to replace Cami because no one could do that, but to have someone there for her. Throughout school, she'd had many 'boy' friends that were like a brother to her and still to this day she has remained close with all of them. She wondered if the news that she'd disappeared again was kept secret or if everyone was searching for her. She felt a little guilty being that close to home and not reaching out, but her gut was telling her to trust Levi and that the only way to keep them all safe was to stay away for now.

Her mind returned to the earlier conversation about what the men wanted from her. She didn't have anything with her when they found her, at least nothing that she knew of. And at the hospital, her dirty clothes and belongings were in a bag, but she emptied that when she got home and again there wasn't anything out of the ordinary there.

Levi walked ahead of her and the two of them searched the woods. Thankfully, the search came up empty, no new bodies that day. They reached the spot where they had dumped her. She stared into the muddy puddle as the memories resurfaced. It seemed so long ago and so much had happened since then. Maybe it was a good thing realizing it didn't feel as traumatic seeing it again.

"That's where I was dumped. As far as I know, I didn't have anything with me just my clothes."

Levi walked to the area and squatted down by the puddle. He fished around in the water but didn't find anything. He continued his search all around the area. He was frustrated when he came up empty and the question of what was in it for him came to her mind again. He was in really good shape, and she estimated him to be in his early thirties. Maybe he was working for the FBI or the CIA. She started to imagine all kinds of things like maybe he was an undercover agent. How did he know that she was going to go into that particular tattoo shop at the exact time? There were so many questions and few answers.

They expanded their search to the area around the puddle. He suggested that she go back to the truck and rest, but she ignored him and continued to help with the search. If they could find something, she could put all of this past her and go home to Deacon. She was surprised that he would allow her to be out of his reach because she could take off and he'd have to chase after her. The thought had crossed her mind again, but Levi's dire warning kept her there with him.

Once they were finished searching the area, they retired to the truck and sat on the back tailgate. At first the conversation was slow but then they started to talk about finding that flash drive. The only thing she could think of was that maybe there was something in her clothes that she missed. If the men that carjacked her were looking for the flash drive they would've searched her clothing before they dumped her. She wondered, did they shoot her before or after they dumped her body in the puddle? They did take her purse and had her car to salvage through. Since they were still coming for her they must've come up empty there, too.

"They came for me at the hospital, too. When I woke up in the night the curtains were moving and I thought that someone was there but Deacon, who was down the hall by the vending area, said that I was imagining it and that no one was there. After we checked out of the hospital, they called to say that they found Deacon's pocketknife behind the curtain only it wasn't his. Maybe they found what they were looking for but then why would I still be a target?"

Levi listened and agreed that if they'd found something they wouldn't still be hunting her. "I doubt that they were stupid enough to cross these people so I would have to say it's still missing. Is there anything else you can remember, maybe some contact with someone else?"

"No. They grabbed me when I was leaving the nursing home, and all of my stuff was in the car. They have access to everything except the clothes I was wearing." Carsyn yawned as she finished her sentence.

"Why don't you go lay down in the back seat of the truck. I'll stay out here and keep watch. I wish I could say this will all be over soon, but I can't promise you that. I don't know what's going to happen next. I can promise you that I will protect you at all cost and hopefully help you find what they want so you can get back to your life and family."

Carsyn walked to the front of the truck and got into the front seat. She pushed the button to recline the seat and used a shirt he had in the back of the truck as a pillow. The Tylenol was kicking in and her leg had stopped throbbing. She felt a feeling of peace come over her and she slipped into a light sleep. She dreamed of Deacon and their last trip to the beach. *She watched as he applied sunscreen to his legs. He hated the beach, but he was there for her. Cami was floating on a raft in the gulf. She got up and went out to meet her, but the waves became fierce, and she couldn't find Cami. She started to panic and call for her but the sound of the waves crashing on the beach was so loud. She called for Deacon.*

Levi shook her arm, and she woke up. Her forehead glistened from sweat and she looked frightened.

"Hey. Are you alright? You were mumbling in your sleep and moving around anxiously. You seemed really distressed so I thought I should wake you."

She was embarrassed that she talked in her sleep and caused him concern. She hated that dream and wished that she would never have to experience it again but lately it had resurfaced. She wondered what she'd said aloud. She had always talked in her sleep, something she'd inherited from her mother, but lately she was doing it more often.

"Did you decide where to go from here?" She wanted to change the subject.

"I think we need to get to the clothes you were wearing when you were carjacked." He saw the skepticism on her face. "You have to have what they want. It's got to be somewhere in your belongings. We searched the place where you were dumped, and you said that everything you had with you at the hospital was put into a bag for you to take home. I hope that you just overlooked it and it's there waiting to be found. Her arm was still numb from leaning on it while she slept. Her legs were like jelly, but she stood up and steadied herself anyway.

"Okay. Let's go."

He stood there shaking his head. "You know you can't go there. It's too dangerous. What if you run into your husband, then what? Are you willing to put him into danger and drag him out here with us? I can make my way there on foot and get in and out without anyone seeing me. You asked me what I do. That's it. That's what I do. I am good at slipping in and out of places unnoticed. Let me do my job please. Tell me where to go to find the bag and the clothes and I'll get them. Do you have a key hidden outside the house?"

"Deacon just changed all the locks because we realized that my attackers had my keys and all my information."

"What about an alarm?"

Carsyn shifted her body. "He just changed that code too but luckily he told it to me before I left for the weekend. It's ROSIE. That's what we agreed on to name our baby daughter one day." Those words saddened her. "What will you do if Deacon catches you? Promise me he won't get hurt."

"I'm not here to hurt either of you, just help. He won't catch me; I promise you that. I shouldn't be gone long because it'll only take me about ten minutes to get there and ten back. I think you should go and stand inside the wooded area in case someone comes by and finds the truck." He pointed to the right of the church.

Her eyes followed his direction and knew that he was unaware that the area he had pointed out was the area where she'd last seen the veil. Excitement took hold and she almost ran to get there. She waited for Levi to leave before she started to feel around hoping to find the veil again.

CHAPTER THIRTY-SEVEN

Carsyn was exhausted. After Levi walked away, she walked around every inch of that area searching for the veil. She retired back at the truck and waited for him to return. She prayed that Deacon wasn't home, and that Levi could get in and out quickly and unnoticed. She wondered if they were still staying at the rental or if they went back home to their own houses. Her stomach ached at the thought of them going crazy with worry about her.

Cami's sweet face came to mind, and she instinctively smiled. She'd been constantly on her mind and Carsyn knew that eventually she'd have to say goodbye again. Hopefully, this time would be different, and she'd get to say goodbye. Tears formed in the corner of her eyes as waves of old memories rolled on by like credits at the end of a movie. She continued to sit there reliving the memories until the sound of a vehicle pulled into the parking lot.

Levi had tucked the truck behind the church and out of sight so she couldn't see the vehicle from her position. She did as he instructed and headed toward the edge of the woods that way if they noticed the truck she would have time to get away.

She leaned against a tree and anxiously waited. She heard the sound of another vehicle on the highway, but it passed the church and kept going. The sun was high in the sky and the heat stifling. Carsyn wiped the sweat from her forehead. She could hear the voices as they drew closer. From her position she could tell that it was two people, and they were out of the car and walking toward the mausoleum. One of them had flowers in their hand which would suggest that they were going to visit a loved one that was buried there. She kept her guard up and stayed hidden just in case.

Fifteen minutes later, she watched as they walked back to their car and left the parking lot. Her body relaxed and she walked back to the truck just as Levi returned carrying a bag in his hands.

"What happened? Was Deacon there?" She fired off one question after another.

"Slow down. No, Deacon wasn't home, no one was there." He dumped the bag he was holding onto the tailgate. "Are these the clothes you were wearing?"

"Yes some of that is." She noticed that there was another t shirt and a pair of shorts in the mix along with a baseball cap belonging to Deacon.

He knew what she was thinking, "I didn't find anything. We need to get to the hospital and see if maybe it could be there. I won't leave you unprotected, so you have to come along. By now I hope you know that you are not a hostage and that you are free to do what you want. I just needed time to prove to you that you and your family were in danger, and it was best to be away from them. I believe that you agree with me now. I thought you could use the baseball cap to tuck away your hair so you're not so recognizable. Time is running out. My sources tell me that things are heating up and that word on the street is, they are growing very impatient and want everyone to be more aggressive."

"More aggressive? What does that mean?" Carsyn knew before she asked but still wanted him to say it.

"You know what that means. Anyone you have been in contact with since the attack will be a target."

"Who exactly are 'they' anyway?" She knew he wasn't going to tell her.

"We're not going there again. I told you it's for your own safety not to know. God willing we will find what they want, and they will go away and leave you alone. That's the goal right now. Please understand that."

She did understand it but didn't like it. The concern in his voice convinced her to go along with his plans and be cooperative, besides, she didn't have any idea what to do herself. She didn't want to be left alone now that she'd accepted that it was best not to reach out to Deacon. She agreed to go with him.

They arrived at the hospital, and he urged her to stay in the truck. He parked on the street instead of the parking garage in case they needed a quick getaway. Reluctantly she stayed in the truck while he, also wearing a baseball cap, headed through the front doors. The clock in the truck seemed to take forever just to turn to the next minute. She prayed he would find something quickly.

Paranoia caused her to jump every time a car passed her on the street. Her nerves were shot, and her patience strained. She yearned for the peaceful feelings she had when Cami was around. She closed her eyes and imagined her face. Before long, the car filled with Cami's scent and the agitation she felt faded away. She relished in the tranquility that had filled her space. She had finally relaxed. She was so in tune with her visions of Cami she felt like she was sitting right next to her in the truck.

Carsyn was so wrapped up in the familiar memory that the hand that gently touched her shoulder almost went unnoticed. The warmth it brought only added to her tranquil state of mind, so she reached up to touch her shoulder. Her eyes shot open, and her body went into panic mode all at once. Recognition set in and then she jumped across the seat to embrace her sister.

"How are you here?" Carsyn released her sister and frantically looked around the truck, "Wait, am I in danger again?"

"Yes, you are but not immediate danger. Where is Levi? Why are you back at the hospital?"

Carsyn explained everything to Cami and when she was finished, she had questions for her.

"I thought you only showed up when I was in danger but you're here now. Does this mean you won't disappear again?"

Cami shrugged her shoulders with uncertainty. "I don't know." She put her arms around Carsyn and tried to comfort her while she could.

"Levi's been gone a while. Do you think you could go check on him?" She tightened her grip on Cami because she didn't want her to leave but she was worried about Levi.

Cami agreed to find Levi but urged Carsyn to stay low and vigilant while she was gone. Without notice, Cami disappeared, and she was all alone in the truck again. *She's getting good at that.* She wanted to turn on the radio but figured that she needed to be able to hear if someone approached the truck, so she sat there and quietly sang her song.

She had to squinch her eyes to be sure that she was seeing someone running toward the truck. It was Levi. He was running full speed and yelling at the same time. Right behind him was Cami moving just as fast, but her feet weren't touching the ground. Carsyn got into the driver's seat and started the truck. Thank God he left the keys. When he reached the truck, he flung open the passenger door and screamed go! She smashed the accelerator to the floor and took off down the street. He instructed her to take back streets through the neighborhood they were in just in case they were followed.

She drove down several streets before ending up at a playground in the area. She pulled into a spot and shut off the engine. Levi's lip was bleeding, and his face was beet red. He was no longer wearing the baseball cap that he had on when he left her. She gave him a minute to catch his breath.

Finally, he sat up and for a moment was speechless until he saw Cami in the back seat. He jumped out of the truck and held up his hands. He looked like he saw a ghost because he did. He yelled for her to get out of the truck and looked confused when she didn't listen.

"Levi wait. This is my sister Cami. Let me explain."

"Your sister? What do you mean, your sister? You can see her too? You see the woman in the back seat?" He was waiting for her to respond.

"Yes, I see her, she's my sister Cami. Get back in the truck please. It's okay, she won't hurt you."

Levi mumbled a few words and slowly got back into the truck keeping his eyes on Cami at all times. "Your sister?" He didn't understand what was happening and was afraid that he was losing his mind.

"Yes. I know it's crazy but right now I need to know where to go. Levi, look at me not her. Yes she's really here and no I don't know how. But from the looks of your face we need to move.

CHAPTER THIRTY-EIGHT

Levi calmed down and instructed Carsyn to go to a nearby hotel. They needed to regroup and possibly freshen up. When he was at her house he grabbed extra clothes for her to change into and he had always kept a change of his clothes in the truck. As much as he tried to ignore Cami's presence, Carsyn noticed that he couldn't and instead seemed almost mesmerized by her.

He checked them into a hotel room and let her go in and freshen up first while he stayed outside in the truck. She knew that he needed time to digest what had happened and preferred to do that alone.

Inside the hotel room, Carsyn was hesitant to let Cami out of her sight but decided to take a quick shower while she had time. Cami told her she would be there when she was finished. After the shower, Carsyn held her breath until she walked back into the room and Cami was still there. She went to the door to tell Levi that the bathroom was open for him. He showered and when he was finished, he walked in on them talking.

"It's okay. You can come out. I'll try to explain what I know to you. When I was first attacked and left for dead,

Cami appeared to me and helped me. I would've died had she not come. We don't know how or why but she just shows up when I'm in danger." Carsyn went on to detail all the times Cami showed up.

"But you're not in danger right now."

Carsyn smiled. "I know."

Cami spoke up. "I don't remember anything other than my times with Carsyn, so I can't explain how any of this is possible.

"But how did you end up helping me?" He looked over at Carsyn. "If she hadn't shown up at the hospital I would probably be dead. When I got out of the elevator I walked straight to the room you were in. There wasn't a name on the outside of the door, so I assumed it was empty and it was. I searched the room and unfortunately didn't find anything. When I left, I decided to take the stairs and that's when I was attacked. Three men came at me, and we scuffled in the stairwell. I'm embarrassed to say that they had the best of me, that is until she showed up."

"Cami. Her name is Cami."

"Sorry. Cami. Anyway, we were all shocked when she appeared out of nowhere and that gave me time to get away. I do have to confess that I ran faster than I ever had in my life and not only because of the men. You scared the heck out of me." Levi's nervous laugh suggested that he was still uncomfortable with Cami.

Carsyn spoke next. "Cami passed away about two years ago." Her voice shook with grief. "It was unexpected and tragic." She looked at her sister who urged her to go on. "We were on vacation at the beach in Florida. We visited the beach every year for as long as I can remember and after we were married we continued to go with our husbands. Cami's husband was out of the country on another tour, so it was just the three of us."

They sat there in silence and waited for her to compose herself enough to continue. The anguish on her face said it all but she wanted to say it. She needed to say it aloud.

She inhaled and then spit it out. "She drowned. Cami drowned and it was all my fault." The tears started to flow.

"That's not true!" Cami protested

"Yes Cami, it is." She went on. "We were in the gulf only about waist deep. Cami didn't like the water, so we always stayed close to the shore. The only reason we were that far out was because I went that far out. Everything was fine and we were having a good time. Then I felt the current swirl around me and before I knew it we were caught up in a riptide. Cami swept past me, and I tried to grab onto her hand. The water was taking us farther out and we couldn't stop it. It all happened so fast." She looked at Cami. "I reached for you, but you were too far away. At one point, I had your hand, and I was so relieved, but then you let go. You let go Cami! Why did you let go? I had you." Carsyn's voice was raised as she relived that moment.

"I fought harder and finally reached you again. I had your hand again but then someone grabbed my leg and pulled me away from you and you let go. Why? Why would you let go? I tried to push them away and get to you, but they wouldn't let me go. Another man passed me trying to reach you, but you went under. The current was so strong. By that time, several people had gathered on the shore and pulled me to safety. Others went in to help find you and finally someone did. I was horrified as I watched the man walk out of the water with your body limp in his arms. Why did you let go?"

Cami quietly said, "Because we would've both died little sister."

"No. I had your hand and you let go."

"If I hadn't, they wouldn't have been able to reach you. We were too far out, and I saw them coming. I had to let go so that they could reach you."

"But why didn't you fight? They revived you. You were in the hospital recovering! They said you could recover. Why didn't you fight? Why did you leave me? I had to watch you lay there for two weeks intubated and I prayed, Cami. I prayed so hard that you would wake up. Everyone was praying for you. So many people were at the hospital and at church praying for you. I was surprised at how many people were in church and praying just for you. People who didn't go to church were there praying so why didn't he answer us? You were such an amazing person. Everyone loved you. You were so kind and humble. You believed in God and lived your life for him every day. You brought his word to so many people and they all showed up for you. We all prayed for you so why didn't he answer our prayers? I was so angry after you died. You weren't supposed to die. We prayed for you in great numbers, 'when two or more gather in prayer he answers,' but he didn't, you still died. Why did you have to die? It should've been me. You were a much better person than me. I was selfish. I was impatient. You lived by the words, 'God's will be done!' You never missed church; you were so faithful. Why did he take you?" Carsyn needed answers.

"I can't answer that other than it was my time to go. He called me home. I know it was hard on you, but it was his will. Listen to what you said. Apparently my death brought so many people to church and back to God. Maybe that was my purpose in life to bring his people back to him. I know this hurts you to hear but I felt joy when you described the people that came back to God because of me. I'm okay. I would do it all over again if it meant saving you. You're my baby sister Carsyn, please don't be angry with God, I'm not. And I'm here now. Your prayers were answered just not the answer you wanted. Sometimes we just have to give it all to God and trust in his plan." Cami wrapped her arms around her sister. "Listen, I can't sit here and say that I understand any of this, but you have to stop beating yourself up about my death. It was not your fault. And you are a good person. Everyone loves you just as much as they ever loved me. Maybe I'm here now because you are a good person and God wants to ease your sorrow. I don't have the answers and I don't care how I'm here, I'm only glad I am."

Carsyn stood up to gather herself. She apologized to Levi for her outbursts and when she looked up at him he looked away.

He rubbed his eyes turned toward the door and told her she didn't have anything to apologize for. "I'm going make a call and check on things." He felt like they needed time alone.

"Why is he helping you? What's his story?" Cami trusted that Levi wanted to help Carsyn she just didn't know why.

Carsyn was totally spent at that point and needed rest. "I don't know his connection and when I ask he shuts me down. He keeps saying some really bad men are after me, but he won't say why. Just that I have something they want." She laid across the bed and found a comfortable spot to rest. She hadn't planned to fall to sleep but when she opened her eyes she was back in the hospital bed with Deacon by her side.

CHAPTER THIRTY-NINE

The hospital bed was in the same position but this time the chair Deacon was usually sleeping in was empty. As Carsyn's eyes adjusted to the darkness, the room around her came into focus. Worry took over because she didn't know how she got there or if she was even really there. She pinched the skin on her arm and flinched when it hurt.

Cami's voice startled her. "Where are we?"

She jumped then she sat up in the bed. "You're here too. That's different." She looked around the room and her eyes stopped on the curtains.

"Shh!" Carsyn put her finger to her lips. She then used that same finger to point to the curtains. "Someone is behind the curtain. This is when I would have gotten up to go to the door and then Deacon comes into the room from the hall and the man gets away."

Cami's face wrinkled with confusion. "What are you talking about, would have? What's happening?"

"I keep dreaming that I'm back here in the hospital only I don't know if it's a dream. Sometimes I close my eyes and I'm here. Then I close them again and I'm not. When

I was in the hospital after the attack, I woke up in the middle of the night and saw the curtains move but Deacon said that I was dreaming." Both women glanced at the curtain and gasped when it moved.

"Where is Deacon?" Cami looked around for him.

"Well, when it happened before, he had stepped out to check his phone and then went to the snack machine. I woke up and saw the curtain move. I ran toward the door, but someone was coming into the room, so I ducked into the bathroom. That's when Deacon found me in the bathroom and eventually got me back to bed. He checked behind the curtain, but no one was there." She was whispering as she watched the curtain continue to move. "We must have entered the dream when he was already gone this time."

Cami made her way to the curtain and disappeared. The next thing she saw was a man run across the room and the blood had drained from his face. He looked familiar when she saw him, but it took her a few minutes to recall where she'd seen him before. He was one of the EMT's that gave them his uniform so that they could get away unnoticed. She knew he looked suspicious.

Cami reappeared and the two of them found themselves back in the hotel room.

"What just happened?"

"I told you that keeps happening and I don't know why or how. Am I going crazy? Am I delusional?" Carsyn was on the verge of tears again.

"If you are, then I am too because I just experienced that with you."

Carsyn chuckled. "Maybe you are just a delusion. Think about it. You can't explain how or why you are here, and you have no memory of being dead. Don't you find that odd Cami?"

"I don't know about you, but I'm not delusional or a figment of your imagination. And if I were, how would I have jumped from one place to the other with you? I think there is something strange going on and I bet it has to do with whatever it is those men are looking for."

"Levi said it was like a flash drive or something smaller, but I don't have it. I don't know why they think I do. I'm so tired. I can't do this. I just want to go home." Carsyn started to whine.

Cami grabbed her wrist and said, "You can handle this. You are strong! You can't be stopped Carsyn! You can weather this storm! Be the storm!"

"That was you. I wondered where those words came from. They just popped into my mind, and I started to recite them. It was you whispering those words to me."

Carsyn repeated the words again and felt courage replace her fears. Since Cami died, she'd become stronger and more independent every day but still had her moments of weakness. Lately, those moments of weakness were happening more often, and those words pulled her through.

"When I first came back, you couldn't see me, but I could see you. That was difficult watching you and unable to reach out. Then I was able to appear sometimes, but I had no control of when and where. I still don't know how things work, but I do know that lately I am here for you whenever you need, not just when you are in danger." What Cami stopped short of saying was that she had no idea how long she would stay or when it would all stop.

Carsyn was so tired but was afraid to close her eyes. Her mind fused over all the things that were out of her control. She was worried about Deacon, Avery and Nick. What if the dangerous men went after them. Maybe they already had, and she didn't know it yet. That thought sent uncontrollable shivers through her body.

"Cami, what if they have Deacon? What if they hurt him? I'm held up here in this hotel hiding from these men, so they don't hurt me but what about Deacon. I need to know that he's alright. I can't lose him. It would be my fault and I could never forgive myself."

"None of this is your fault. You didn't ask for any of this. Are you sure you don't have what they want? They are putting all their efforts into finding you so they must know something we don't. Start from the beginning and tell me everything that happened leading up to the time you were carjacked. There must be something we're missing. Think, Carsyn. Try to remember."

"I went over it a hundred times in my mind. I left the house early to go to Hobby Lobby to get supplies. I was meeting Avery and the girls over at the nursing home for our weekly scrapbooking class." She looked at Cami and guilt consumed her. "I'm sorry Cami. I know you wanted us to scrapbook together, and I refused."

Cami just smiled. "Carsyn, it's fine. Go on. What else can you remember?"

"When I got to the store, I noticed a white van with two men standing around it and I thought they were staring at me. I tried to ignore them, but I was still rattled. I rushed into the store to get what I needed. A few times I felt like someone was following me, but I just thought it was a coincidence. I was so upset that I slammed right into a man and hurt my shoulder."

Levi pushed open the door and walked into the room. "Did you say you ran into a man?" He rushed to her and grabbed both of her arms. "Think, Carsyn, what did he look like? Did you see anyone else around?" His voice was edgy, and he wanted answers.

"Let go of me." He let her go and she sat back down. "Yes a man slammed into me, or I slammed into him, either way we collided. It happened so fast but now that I think about it he was rushing down the aisle." She stood up. "I bet someone was chasing him. That's it! They weren't there watching me they were there chasing him. He has what they want, not me. Why don't they just find him."

Levi was quiet and the look on his face was somber. "Can you describe the man to me? What did he look like? Was he tall? What color hair? Eyes? Age? Anything you can remember would help."

"He wasn't really tall, maybe five nine or so. It happened so fast Levi, I didn't get a good look at him. He was an older man in his early fifty's maybe."

He looked uncomfortable as he digested her words. He reached into his wallet and pulled out a photo. "Is this the man?"

Carsyn eyes widened as she looked at the photo.

Levi's phone pinged with a message. He looked down at the words, "Move now!"

He grabbed the photo from her hands, told her to grab her stuff, and headed to the door. "We have to move now! They found us!"

CHAPTER FORTY

They left the hotel and headed back in the direction of Crown Point. "Are we going back to the church? What if they are waiting there for us?"

"They're not there." Levi's answer was short.

"How do you know? We could be walking right into their hands. Why don't we just go to the police? We could call Detective Stevens for help. Levi, how do you know they're not at the church?"

"Because they're at your house!" He regretted the words the minute they left his lips.

Carsyn's world started to spin out of control. At first she was too shocked to speak, then she didn't know what to say. They're at my house. "Oh my God! What if Deacon's there! What if he comes home when they're still there? We have to go to my house. They want me not Deacon! We have to go to my house now!" She yelled at Levi to listen to her.

Levi kept driving. He was beating himself up for saying that to her. He should've kept his mouth shut. "Deacon's not home." He noticed that she looked like she was going to hyperventilate. "Carsyn, look at me. Did you hear what I said, he's not there. We're going back to the church. Listen I have a guy on the inside. I promise you, Deacon's not there.

"Where's Cami? Where did she go? She was right there."

Levi glanced at the back seat. He still wasn't comfortable with the idea of a ghost around, but he wondered the same thing. "She was just there a minute ago. Maybe she went on ahead to check things out for us. To make sure it was safe. She said she was here to protect you so that's probably what she's doing." He didn't want Carsyn to become more upset than she already was.

They arrived at the church and Levi pulled the truck close to the back of the church like he had done before. She jumped out first and called for Cami. She walked around in circles, and it looked like she was trying to summon her.

After she called out to Cami several times, she finally appeared. Carsyn rushed into her arms almost knocking her down. She recalled the first time she saw Cami her hands went right through her. She was glad that Cami learned how to get into solid form instead of just a spirit.

"Where were you? I thought you were going to be here when we got here."

"I went to your house. Don't worry, they didn't see me. Deacon's not there. They are going through your clothes and dresser drawers looking for something. They are some scary looking characters, Carsyn. You do not want to mess with them."

"You said you have someone on the inside. Do you know who these men are? Did you work for them? Are you still working for them?" Carsyn wanted the truth.

"Yes, I do have someone on the inside. I wouldn't have said that if it wasn't true. Look, it's a long story." He wasn't ready to tell her everything yet.

"What else do we have besides time?" She stood tall challenging him.

"Okay. You might want to sit down for this one. No. I don't work for them, but my brother n law did, and he worked for them until he realized what they really wanted from him. He was a computer scientist and a professor at Loyola University in New Orleans."

"Why would he work for people like that? What did they want him to do?"

Levi ignored her questions and continued. "He was working on developing new technology for them over the last few months. They had their own scientists working alongside him and he found out they were manipulating him and had other ideas for the use of the technology. When he realized the trouble he was in he contacted me. They must've had his phone bugged because he called me and said he was afraid for his life. He was going to grab my sister and meet me." His expression turned dark. "They never showed up."

She wasn't expecting him to say that. Her tone softened and she reached out to touch his hand.

"I'm so sorry. Are they still missing?"

After he gathered his emotions he said, "No. He's dead and she's in the hospital fighting for her life."

Cami got between them and informed them that they had company. They looked up and saw several black cars drive up in the parking lot. It wouldn't take long to find them and there was no way they could outrun them.

Cami looked at Carsyn and without a word Carsyn knew what she was thinking. Cami grabbed Carsyn's hand while Carsyn grabbed Levi's and they ran toward the woods. The veil appeared and shimmered in front of their eyes inviting them to enter. Before Levi could object, Cami leaped forward, and they all disappeared into the veil.

Carsyn watched as Levi bounced to his feet ready for action looking back and forth in every direction. His eyes were wide and wild, but she wasn't sure if it was from fear or the disbelief of what had just happened.

He tried to find his words but just kept mumbling. She understood what he was feeling because the first time she went through the veil, she was stunned and speechless. The first time was when she saw Cami and was overjoyed to see her sister. As she remembered the second time her body stiffened. She slowly canvassed the area, and it was as beautiful and peaceful as she remembered but she also recalled how quickly that could change in that world.

Levi finally found his voice. "What was that? Where are we?" He looked back toward the place they'd traveled through, and the veil was gone. He looked over at the other two women and noticed that they were calm and familiar with the place, "You've been here before? Is it safe?"

"Yes. This is where I first saw Cami. She yanked me in without any warning. I was just as stunned as you and before you ask, no we don't know how or why it appears, but it just does.

His eyes fell upon Cami. "You have no explanation for any of this?"

Cami stood stern. "No, I don't. I could feel that my sister was in trouble and needed help. I didn't even know how to cross through the veil at first. As time passes, I become stronger and discover all kinds of new things I can do."

Levi marveled at the beauty of the place while Cami spoke. "This is unbelievable."

Carsyn didn't want to burst his bubble, but she knew just how dangerous and ugly it could get and felt she needed to warn him. She kept looking in the distance as she spoke.

"It is beautiful but that can change quickly. There are things here, really ugly things that you don't want to see." Her eyes widened and her voice fell to a whisper.

He followed her stare and noticed dark skies in the distance. "What do you mean by ugly?" He continued to stare as the darkness moved toward them. "Carsyn!" He yelled for her to answer and when she didn't he understood that he was going to find out soon enough.

"We can't stay here." Cami walked toward the missing veil looking for the way back.

Before they could get out, the dark sky descended on them, and a dust storm was rolling closer. Carsyn and Levi took cover behind a large tree and huddled together. The terror on her face explained that things were about to get really bad.

"Oh my God! They're coming. We have to get out of here. They're coming." Carsyn squeezed her eyes closed as she braced for the attack.

"Who? Carsyn,, who's coming?" The dust was so thick he had trouble breathing. He closed his eyes to shield them as well.

The thoughts of the skeleton people from the last time she was there slammed into her mind. "The skeleton people."

Just as she spoke the words, tall black skeletal things rose from the ground.

"This is insane. This can't be real. What do we do?" Levi stood up.

Carsyn started to hum her song to distract herself from what was about to happen. The sky thundered and the sand gusted with the wind. She flinched when she felt the sand from the storm reach her arm. She focused her mind on the words of her song and then suddenly everything stopped. They slowly got up and looked around for any threat, but it had all disappeared, and the landscape was back to the beautiful tranquil place it was when they got there.

Levi said it again. "This is insane."

CHAPTER FORTY-ONE

Instead of jumping back through the veil right away they decided to wait just in case the men were still there looking for them. Too afraid to venture out, they huddled near the area they were familiar with and waited.

"I'm sorry about your brother n law and sister." She waited and let her sympathetic words linger. "Are they from this area?"

Levi shook his head.

"And you think the men after me are responsible?" She already knew the answer.

"I know they are. And that's why I keep telling you that they're dangerous and will stop at nothing to get what they want." He started pacing, ready to move on.

Cami announced that she would go through the veil and see if it were safe to return. Carsyn didn't want her to leave but instead wanted them all to go together.

"You need to stay here for now. You won't be alone because Levi will be with you." Cami tried to reason with her.

Carsyn started to panic again as her fears resurfaced. She didn't want to stay there any longer than she had to, and she thought it was safer to stay together. "We can all go together and if they're still there you can spook them like you did before. I don't want to stay here without you Cami. What if those things come back?" The more she spoke the shakier her voice became. As if on cue, the skies darkened in the distance and the wind picked up.

"Oh my God! See. They're coming again. We have to leave here now." Carsyn latched onto Cami and urged her to move.

Levi nodded to Cami that he agreed and the three of them, with Cami in the lead, leaped back through the veil. There was no confusion this time as to where they had landed because all three plunged into the Intercoastal Canal that flowed behind the wooded area of the church. They swam to the muddy bank and climbed onto the dry land. They sat there catching their breath and gathering their bearings. Before too long the sound of branches snapping made its way to them.

They stayed low to the ground and moved away from the sound but the sound of branches snapping from the direction they were going in told them that the threat was coming from both sides.

"They must've split up. Maybe we should split up. I can distract them while you get away." Carsyn could barely hear his voice.

"No." She shook him off.

"We don't have a choice. Cami won't be able to scare them all if they are separated. Slip back down into the water and hang close to the bank. I'll run straight ahead through the woods and hopefully they'll follow me. Cami can stay by you in case they come your way." He saw the terror in her eyes. "It's the only way. I can't let them get to you."

Tears were streaming down Carsyn's face. She didn't want to be separated and she feared what they would do to Levi when they caught him. She looked to Cami for help, but she shook her head acknowledging that she agreed with Levi.

"Time to adult up little sister." Cami hated seeing Carsyn upset but thought it was best to follow Levi's plan. "You can do this. You are strong."

Reluctantly, she followed Levi's suggestion slipping back into the water and eventually found an area close to the bank to lean against. Cami stayed near her and once she was hidden, motioned to Levi to go.

She heard his footsteps as he rushed through the brush and trees leading them away from her and before long she heard voices yelling for him to stop. After a while, footsteps converged on the area of land just above where she was hiding. She couldn't tell how many men were there, but it sounded like several. It was probably an hour before she heard doors open and close and figured they were finally leaving the area.

"What are we going to do now? I shouldn't have let him do that. What if they kill him Cami? We have to help him. Please, see what's going on." Cami hesitated. "I don't want to leave you alone."

"Hurry, Cami. Just float on over there and see what happened to Levi. They must have him. They are going to kill him if we don't help. You're a ghost so go check it out. That's kinda your thing isn't it. They can't see you unless you want them to so you can check it out and get back here quickly." Carsyn didn't want to be alone but if they lost Levi she would be anyway. "Go."

Cami smiled at her baby sister then disappeared.

When Cami materialized again, Carsyn had climbed out of the water and was sitting against a tree looking deflated. She lit up when she saw the vision of her sister return.

"Did you see Levi? Is he alright?"

"Yes. He's in the back of one of the cars. Carsyn, there are five cars here and I counted about fifteen men. There's nothing we can do, it's too many of them."

Carsyn laughed and Cami didn't find that amusing. "Are you laughing? This is serious!" Cami scolded her sister.

"I just think it's funny when you said there were too many of them as if I could do something even if it was just one man. I'm sitting here out of breath with a hurt shoulder and a wounded leg. And you, well we have no idea of what you are capable. I know this is serious, but you have to admit we are a pair." She cracked a smile at her.

"I think you need to go with them and see where they bring Levi. I don't know what we could do but if we don't know where they take him then there is nothing we can do. I'll be alright. Did you see anyone else in the woods?"

"No, I checked the entire area out before I came back here."

"Okay, you go with Levi and after ya'll leave, I'll go to the truck and wait there for you to come back. I love you, Cami. I'm glad you're here." Carsyn relaxed against the tree and closed her eyes. She was so tired and really needed some Tylenol.

After Cami left, she sat back and thought about the past few days. She thought that losing Cami was the worst thing that could have ever happened to her, and it still was but she never dreamed that she and Deacon would be in danger and that she might lose him as well. Losing both of them would be the worst thing to ever happen to her. She tried to push those awful thoughts aside and think about her next move.

When she thought that enough time had passed, she made her way back to the truck and grabbed the bottle of Tylenol. She was grateful that it was a large bottle because she was going to need them. She swallowed three pills and waited for the effects to kick in.

She wondered where they were taking Levi. It had been about 30 minutes and Cami still wasn't back. She thought about reaching out to Deacon, she really wanted to, but she was afraid. Chances were that wherever Deacon was Nick and Avery were with him because they wouldn't want him to be alone. Her heart ached for them because they had to be out of their minds with worry about her. As much as she wanted to ease their pain, she knew that she needed to do this on her own. Well, she was with Cami of course but they couldn't harm her, at least she didn't think they could.

She also wondered if Levi knew that Cami was with him. Most people can't see her, but he could, so hopefully it brought him some comfort knowing she was there. He seemed tough, but everyone gets scared sometimes and if the men were as dangerous as he said they were, then he was scared.

Cars continued to pass on the street in front of the church, and she held her breath each time and prayed that they would keep going. Sitting there alone and worried allowed her mind to single in on losing Cami again and as hard as she tried to surpass the unwanted thoughts, they kept resurfacing.

All the old feelings came flooding back and she was filled with grief and sorrow as raw as the day it all happened. Of course, everyone offered encouraging words and told her that only time would heal her. They told her that, "We can't begin to understand God's plan, but it was his will." What they don't say is, "You will think about her almost every minute of every day and even when you are preoccupied, the grief will sneak back in and take over." They don't say, "That all of her memories include Cami and are all attached to the grief she felt when she died, and that everything she did would bring with it, guilt, that God didn't take her instead." Carsyn was hunched over, and tears were flowing like a raging river as she sobbed uncontrollably. She struggled to catch her breath, but she was too far gone. Her heart felt like it had been ripped into a million pieces, just like the day it all happened, and she knew that no matter what anyone said, it would never be whole again. She would put on a happy face for Deacon, her friends and family and go through the motions of life, but she accepted a long time ago that deep down in her heart and soul there was a darkness that would never heal. A nightmare that she would never wake up from. A yearning that would never be satisfied.

CHAPTER FORTY-TWO

Carsyn was still there on the ground sobbing uncontrollably when Cami reappeared. Her hands had covered her swollen eyes as she tried to fight off the force of her emotions that continued to rule her thoughts. She was muttering aloud, and her words were incoherent. She was unaware that Cami had returned.

Cami hated to interrupt her, but she knew her sister and that her crying could go on for a while and they didn't have time to waste. "Carsyn."

The abrupt sound of Cami's voice startled her, causing her to scream. She tried to dry her eyes with her shirt, but the tears were still rolling. She inhaled deeply and stood up to regain her composure.

"I didn't hear you come back. Did you find Levi?" She'd hoped that Cami wouldn't want to talk about the fact that she was crying like a baby.

"Yes. They took him to an old, abandoned building near Joe's Landing in Barataria."

"That's only about ten miles from here. What took you so long?" Carsyn was beginning to feel normal again.

"What took so long? I've only been gone for about a half an hour. I stayed with him until they eventually took him out of the car and locked him in a room."

"Did he see you? Cami, did he know you were there? Did they hurt him?"

"Yes. He saw me when I popped into the car with him before they left the parking lot. He shook his head and I think he was somehow trying to tell me not to leave you alone, but he didn't speak. Aside from being a little roughed up from when they grabbed him, he didn't look hurt. Once they locked him in the room, he urged me to come back and protect you. He said that he would be fine but that you needed me more."

"What are we going to do?" Carsyn was sick to her stomach at the thought of abandoning him.

"I checked out the place and it's pretty shabby. There are entrances all around the building. That's why I waited. All of the cars except one left the area and the two men from that car were standing guard at the front door. I think they might be coming back here to look for you again. We need to get out of here."

Carsyn headed to the truck.

"Whoa. What are you doing? You can't take the truck. They'll be looking for you and they know this truck."

"Do you know how to hot wire a car?" She stared dead into Cami's eyes.

Cami laughed but quickly realized that she was serious. "No, Carsyn. No! We are getting out of here and going to find someplace safe for you to hide out for a while."

There were houses near the church and she was sure she could find a car. There's no way she was going to leave Levi there.

Cami grabbed Carsyn's arm. "Stop. It's too dangerous." She held onto to her arm refusing to let go. "I said no! Now stop acting like a child and listen."

"You sound like mom!" Carsyn tried to free herself from the grip, but she couldn't.

"Well that's because you are acting like a child and not thinking straight. You always do that. You act before you think and end up getting into a bigger mess. What are you going to do, go there with all guns blazing. Oh wait, you don't have a gun. Do you at least have a weapon, maybe a screwdriver from Levi's glovebox? You're being ridiculous and are going to get both you and Levi hurt or worse killed." Cami let go of her arm.

Carsyn's face was on fire as she listened to the words her sister was shouting at her. *Who does she think she is? She's not my mother!* She wanted to scream back at her but instead calmly said, "No, I don't have a gun, I don't need a gun. I have you." She turned and walked toward the wooded area on side of the church that led to the nearby houses.

"Stop. What do you think I can do? I can't protect you from a bullet." She jumped in front of Carsyn. "I don't know if I can protect you baby sister. Please don't do this." Cami saw the look in her eyes and knew that she'd already made up her mind. *I knew you were strong little sister.* She just hoped she had a plan.

She made her way to one of the houses and there, parked in the driveway was a small Honda. She used the house as cover and walked over to the car. She said a quick prayer and tried the door handle. It clicked open and she slid onto the seat. Cami materialized next to her and just shook her head.

"Are we really doing this? What now? Don't look at me. I have never hotwired a car before."

Carsyn sat for a minute then started to search the car. By pure miracle, when she pulled on the sun visor, a key dropped into her lap. She looked at it with disbelief.

"You gotta be kidding me. Who leaves their keys in the car anymore? You were always the luckiest person I knew."

"If I were the luckiest person, you would still be alive and here with me."

Cami felt horrible but Carsyn was also known for being dramatic. "I am here with you, so I guess you still are the luckiest person I know." She wanted to lighten the mood after her last comment, and it worked.

They both laughed at each other until Carsyn turned over the engine. She backed out of the driveway and headed toward the bridge that would take them to Levi. Cami looked back and reported that, thankfully, no one noticed that their car had just been stolen.

"Look in that glove box and see if there is anything we can use, like maybe a screwdriver." Carsyn was still mad at Cami for being so mean earlier.

Cami ignored the sarcasm and opened the glove box. The distorted look on her face forced Carsyn to look down to see what she was seeing. Her eyes settled on a small gun tucked in the corner.

Growing up in Crown Point, they were both familiar with guns because their father took them hunting and fishing all the time. That was some of her favorite memories because her father was usually busy working hard to provide a good life for them but on those days they had his full attention. They eventually explored every inch of Crown Point, not only the land but the bayou as well. She missed her father and at that moment was grateful that he taught them to shoot a gun.

Carsyn noticed that Cami was apprehensive because she sat there staring at the gun. "I don't think this is a good idea little sister. What if you have to use this gun? Are you prepared to live with the consequences or possibly die from them?"

She hadn't thought about that. She hadn't had time to. But her life was in danger as well as her family and she would do whatever needed to be done. Her stomach churned at the thought of shooting someone or worse killing them. However, she was glad to have a weapon for self-defense if need be.

She pushed back the uncomfortable thoughts and said, "We may not even need the gun. You said there were several entrances, so we can go in and find Levi without them even noticing us. Besides, we have a more powerful weapon anyway – you. I was thinking, when we get close we can park the car and walk the rest of the way. You can fly ahead of me to make sure everything is clear. Then when we get there you can fly, or do whatever it is you do, and see if Levi is alone and how we get to him. Easy right?"

Cami had forgotten how Carsyn always thought she could do everything and that it was always gonna be easy. She rolled her eyes at her childish mentality. Instead of yelling at her she calmly said, "I don't think this is going to be easy. I just pray that we get in, get Levi, then get out of there without anyone getting hurt."

Being ever vigilant of their surroundings, they drove in silence and stared out the windows. The two lane road ran along side of the bayou and was lined with beautiful yellow wildflowers. Carsyn smiled because she loved yellow flowers.

"I love yellow flowers" Cami said in a whisper.

"So do I." Carsyn had forgotten that Cami loved the wildflowers, too. "I guess we have that in common. We both love the color yellow."

"Do you not remember that mom loved yellow flowers. Any chance she got, she would take us into a field of yellow flowers around the house, and we would hold hands, dance around in a circle and sing her favorite song, Que Sera, Sera by Doris Day. She loved her music and yellow flowers. My favorite color is green, well it was green." Cami's voice drifted off.

"I remember, but I just thought that we all loved yellow flowers because we loved the color yellow. I'm sorry I didn't know your favorite color." Carsyn reached out and covered Cami's hand with her own.

"Recently, I discovered a different version of Que Sera, Sera by Sly & The Family Stone. Remind me later to play it for you." Carsyn knew they were getting close and stiffened as she thought of the danger they were facing. "I love you Cami. I know I haven't said that enough and I just wanted to make sure that you know. A part of me died with you big sister and that void will never be replaced or heal. And that's okay because you are a part of everything I do and are always with me. I'm really anxious for all of this to be over, but what if that means losing you again? I don't want to do that." Tears stung her eyes again as she faced the prospect of losing Cami again.

"Who knows what's to be. But think of all the fun we can have if I stay around."

They both forced a giggle then geared up for what was to come. She parked the car and they quietly got out, careful not to make noise as they closed the doors. There was a field between them and the building. Carsyn smiled to herself and felt reassured because they were walking to the building through a field of yellow wildflowers. When they got closer, Cami went to see if anything had changed with Levi's situation from when she was there before.

She reappeared next to Carsyn, who jumped from fright, and reported that things were the same.

"Shoot Cami! You scared me! I'll never get used to you popping in and out. Can't you make some kind of noise or give me a signal to prepare me when you're going to appear? It's really scary you know." Carsyn's heart was already pumping out of her chest because of the tense situation, and she didn't need anything else to scare her on top of that. "A little notice would be nice."

Cami was blindsided by her baby sisters bi-polar behavior. "You just said you loved me and can't live without me and didn't want to lose me all over again and then you complain that I scared you. Listen to yourself. We don't have time for this."

They were standing by the back entrance of the building. It was quiet and hidden by overgrown trees and brush and of course yellow wildflowers. Her stomach knotted and her body tingled with anticipation. She closed her eyes and prayed. She prayed that they would find Levi and that no one would get hurt. She prayed that Cami would still be there after it was over and then she prayed that God's Will Be Done.

CHAPTER FORTY-THREE

Carsyn stood by the back door and waited for Cami to come back, scare her, and say that the coast was clear. She felt sluggish and disorientated and remembered that she hadn't eaten much lately. She rubbed her eyes for clarity and when she opened them again she was back in the hospital.

"No! Not now! No! I can't be here. I have to save Levi!" She rubbed her eyes harder and opened them to find she was still in the hospital. She rubbed again and called for Cami. She repeated the process a few more times but nothing worked. She refused to accept defeat and resorted to the only thing that gave her comfort in times of trouble. She started to sing her song in her mind. She cried for Levi. She cried for Cami. She sang louder and the tears came faster. She stopped suddenly when she heard someone join in. *Cami! Cami I need you.*

Cami appeared and held out her hand. "I'm here. What happened to you? How did you get back here? Why'd you leave?" Cami held onto her hands.

"I don't know. I don't know what to do. We have to get to Levi." She closed her eyes and felt Cami pull.

Next thing she knew, they had tumbled to the ground behind the building. Carsyn landed on her shoulder and whimpered. She could feel a small bump and knew that it was hurt and bruised from before. She stood up and used her other arm to hold it close to her body for support. *Maybe I dislocated it this time.* She slowly opened the door trying to minimize the squeaking sound from being rusty.

Cami went ahead to show her the way to Levi. The building was empty and even though it looked small from the outside, it was very spacious and open on the inside. They stayed close to the inner walls and walked lightly. The hallway got darker the farther they walked but her eyes adjusted.

Cami stopped at a door and motioned that it was where Levi was being held. It was a large storage room that was locked from the outside. As luck was still on their side, the key was in the lock, so she turned it and listened as the door squeaked as well. She opened it slowly and squeezed in once she had enough space. Levi was standing there waiting for her because Cami had let him know they were there.

"What are you doing here? Are you crazy! This is too dangerous. I told you not to worry about me." He was furious that she had risked her life for him.

"Look, you didn't leave me and I'm not going to leave you." She walked further into the room still holding her shoulder.

Cami interrupted them and suggested that they save all of that for later and that they should hurry up. She was going ahead to make sure that the two men were still outside and out of the way so that they could leave safely.

Levi stared at Carsyn. She looked tired and moved slowly when she walked. "Did you hurt your leg again?"

"I don't think so." She leaned against the wall and examined her leg for signs of blood. There was one chair in the middle of the room, and he helped her get settled into it while they waited on Cami to return.

"I think I might have dislocated my shoulder though. It really hurts and I know it was bruised from before but now it's worse. I must've landed on a rock or something because I have a small bump developing like a goose egg you get when you hit something." She stood up ready to move.

Levi lifted her sleeve and saw the bump she was talking about and confirmed that it was really bruised. He took her arm in his hands, and she flinched when he moved it. He looked her in the eyes apologetically and before she realized he popped her shoulder back into place. Her legs gave out and she fell into his arms as she tried to stifle her screams.

"I'm sorry love, but that was the only way to do it. How does it feel now?"

She sat back down in the chair and caught her breath. She lifted her arm and moved it around in circles. "That feels much better, just still really sore. How'd you learn to do that?"

Before he could answer, Cami popped back into the room looking terrified. "We gotta go now. Two more cars just pulled up and they're heading for the front door."

They didn't have time to worry about the squeaky door, so they flung it open and ran to the back of the building. They made it safely out the door and headed for the field. They heard the doors open and then the sound of bullets flying through the air. They dove forward taking cover in the tall overgrown grass. Cami was floating above them holding the gun in her hand. Her face was riddled with uncertainty, and she looked confused.

"Toss me the gun!" Cami looked down when she heard Levi's voice. "Cami! Toss me the gun!"

She snapped into action, tossed the gun to Levi then disappeared.

"Cami! Where are you?" Carsyn was crawling behind Levi trying to find a safe place to stop. She noticed drops of blood on some of the grass as they passed. She felt her leg and it was dry. She slowed down and watched as Levi continued to crawl leaving a trail of blood behind him.

"Levi, you're bleeding. We have to stop. You're hurt."

"Don't you dare stop Carsyn!" He yelled at her but then softened his tone. "I'm okay love. It's just a nick. Keep moving. How did ya'll get here, my truck?"

She kept moving but was sure by the amount of blood she was seeing that it was more than a nick.

"No, Cami said it was too dangerous. We stole a car. We parked on the other side of this field. We're almost there."

"You stole a car?" He wasn't surprised because he knew from the beginning that she was going to be trouble and that she was spunky. He grinned to himself. He thought about what she'd been through and how she kept getting back up. Even with a dislocated, bruised shoulder… "Wait! That's it!"

The sound of the brush rustled behind them, and they were running out of time. They were both injured and tired, but they picked up the pace almost dragging their bodies behind them. A yell rang out first! Then another high pitched scream. Gunshots rang out but this time they weren't the target.

"Cami." They both said her name at the same time. They shuffled on and finally reached the other side. They heard engines start and braced for the battle that was coming their way.

The car was parked just where she'd left it, but the other vehicles were already in pursuit, so they had to leave it behind. They decided to double back toward the building and prayed that everyone had joined in the chase. They stayed quiet and low to the ground and made their way past the building to a few houses that were along the bayou. Thankfully, almost everyone that lived in the area had a boat tied up to their dock ready to go.

They found a pirogue that was pulled up onto the bank and decided it was their best option. They noticed that there were no paddles, so they entered the boat shed hoping to push their luck a little further. Aside from fishing gear, crab traps and a few life jackets laying around, there was nothing they could use as a paddle. Levi slipped into the boat that was housed in the boat shed and searched the compartments. Finally, he found one oar and decided that would have to do.

Carsyn was worried about the amount of blood seeping from Levi, but he just brushed her off again. She grabbed two life vest and an old rag and followed him to the pirogue. He helped her climb in then pushed the pirogue off the bank before jumping in himself. The pirogue rocked back and forth until they settled, and it found a balance. They could see across the bayou to the other side, to safety, but were afraid to be out in the open, exposed to the men that were hunting them. Instead, they drifted along the bank and hoped to get far enough up the bayou before they crossed to safety even if it was temporary.

CHAPTER FORTY-FOUR

The bayou traffic was light, so the boat glided easily with the use of one ore. They were both worn, and welcomed a brief break from danger and chaos. Carsyn tossed the towel to Levi and nodded to his side. He glared down at his bloody shirt and cursed under his breath. He leaned forward and grabbed a rope that was on the floor of the boat. He lifted his shirt, held the towel against his skin and attempted to use the rope to secure it. He fumbled for a few seconds before Carsyn scooted over to help.

All of a sudden, there was a loud thump that rocked the already tipsy pirogue and startled both of them. Carsyn was relieved to see that it was Cami and that she was back with them.

"Where were you? I was starting to worry that you left again." She questioned her sister while she helped bandage Levi's wound.

"Wow! How about, 'I'm glad you're okay, Cami' or maybe even a 'thank you' would be nice."

She looked up from her nursing chore and saw that her sister was upset. "What's your problem? I didn't worry that much about your safety because, you know, you're…" Carsyn felt bad the minute she started the sentence. "What I mean is that I was worried about you because I thought something had happened and that you had left again. I hadn't thought about you getting hurt. Is that a thing? Oh my God Cami, can they hurt you? Are you hurt?" Her demeanor changed when that idea surfaced. The blood drained from her checks, and she turned white as a ghost. She finished with Levi and turned to Cami for an answer.

The anger Cami felt faded, and she felt guilty for worrying Carsyn. "I really don't know what could happen, but I don't think they can hurt me. I'm quite sure that bullets flew at me, probably through me, and I wasn't injured. In fact I know that they flew through me because at one point I was sandwiched between two of the men and when they fired, they shot each other. There are still several men looking for ya'll. I took care of the one's that were on foot but then came straight over here to check on ya'll. I did see the cars go back toward the bridge slowly and made it to the other side still searching for ya'll. They think that their men on foot have that ground area covered but it won't take them long to figure out something's wrong when they don't report in. Ya'll don't have a lot of time, so I hope there's a plan?"

Levi had returned to using the oar to push them along while taking Cami's words of urgency seriously. He knew the type of men they were up against and was trying to stay optimistic. "Eventually, we'll have to cross the bayou hopefully we can stay under the radar." He looked both up and down the bayou for shelter. There were a few trawling boats getting ready to go out and a couple of recreational boats in the distance. His plan was to wait for them to get in the area then ride along side of them for shelter.

The tall grass a few feet behind the boat rustled and caught Levi's attention. Before his mind registered what the sound represented, the rapid gunfire began "Get down!" He jumped on top of Carsyn and tried to cover her with his body but the sudden movement in the pirogue was too much and it flipped over hurling them into the muddy bayou water.

Cami yelled that she was going after them.

Carsyn screamed before she went under.

Levi surfaced quickly and grabbed onto the capsized pirogue.

Bullets continued to riddle the area.

Then it was all quiet again.

Carsyn was hanging onto a cypress knee that was jutting out into the bayou. Her head was tucked low, and she remained motionless. She saw Levi floating alongside of the boat and when he reached her, he let the boat float away. Neither of them spoke. They watched as one of the trawl boats approached. He shook his head "no" to her and she agreed. As much as she wanted to scream for help, the last thing she wanted was to cause someone else to get hurt. She knew at that moment they were on their own.

"Listen to me. Carsyn. We don't have a lot of time. I know what they want from you, and I now know its location. I told you that they killed my brother n law and left my sister to die." His words were strained.

"I'm sorry Levi. I pray that your sister will be alright."

"Thank you but there's more. The man that bumped into you at the Hobby Lobby was my brother n law. He was running from these men when he bumped into you trying to get away"

She listened but his words didn't register and subconsciously rubbed her shoulder as she remembered the incident.

He knew that they were on to him and didn't know what to do. He called me and we planned to meet but like I said earlier, he didn't show up." He saw the light bulb in her mind make the connection and waited for her to catch up to what he was saying.

"They think he gave something to me. The men in the parking lot were after him not me. But they have all of my belongings and I'm sure they searched me before they left me for dead." Shock was written all over her face.

"When he came out of the store they grabbed him and eventually killed him. They had taken my sister, shot her and left her for dead in the wooded area where you were dumped."

When this revelation registered she gasped. "The woman in the woods. That was your sister. We found your sister?" Her world suddenly began spinning as the events twirled around in her mind.

Bullets started to pound the area again and this time they pulled themselves out of the water and onto the bank attempting to crawl to safety. Levi jumped to his feet and pulled her up beside him. They ran back into the woods away from the water and the bullets sprayed the area as they ran.

"Listen to me carefully. You have what they want. They won't kill you because you have what they want. You need to get away. Get to safety and call Detective Stevens. He will help you. He's one of us and you can trust him."

"Why are you telling me that now?" Carsyn was surprised by this information.

"Because they are going to catch us. The bullets aren't meant to kill us but to drive us in their direction. They want you. They need what you have." Cami reappeared and he produced an idea. "Can you appear to anyone? Cami, do you have the ability to appear to anyone you want?"

"I think so. It doesn't always work but I'm getting better at it."

"Carsyn you need to stay put." He glanced around and found a place for her to hide. "Cami will come with me, revealing herself to them, so that they will think it's you. That'll give you some time to get away." He saw the fright in her eyes. "She'll be okay. You heard what she said, bullets went through her body. And once you've had time to get away, she'll come to you." Before she could respond Levi pushed her down into a pocket in the earth created by a toppled tree.

Cami looked down and shook her head in apology before speaking. "Sorry Carsyn, but I agree with Levi. This is the only way to keep you safe."

She began to cry as she pleaded with them to stop. She was terrified of being left alone, but she believed what Levi said and knew they wouldn't kill her but what about him? What would keep them from killing Levi? She watched them run away from her and listened as the bullets landed in that direction.

Levi looked back over his shoulder and yelled. "Stay hidden! Just stay hidden!."

She pleaded with them again and the last thing she heard was, "Sing. Baby Sister. Sing. Quietly sing our song. It'll be okay."

CHAPTER FORTY-FIVE

Her ears zeroed in on the echo of bullets that followed Levi and Cami away from her hiding spot. She cringed to know that they were risking their lives to save her. Again. The information Levi had just laid on her was settling in and she was trying to make sense of it all. She thought about the woman she and Avery found in the woods. She was in critical condition when they found her, probably just minutes from death, and he said she was still fighting for her life.

Levi also indicated that he knew what they were after and where it was located, but their time ran out before he could explain it all to her. She stood up and started to run after them. She needed to know what he knew. How was she going to stop them if she couldn't find what they wanted? He said they wanted her alive but for how long? Would they finally give up and kill her? Were they going to torture her? She decided that she wasn't going to stick around and find out.

She made her way back to the boat shed where they found the oar and climbed into the boat. She slid below the back seat and ducked under the cover of a blanket.

She was so tired that she had to fight to stay awake. She needed to find a way to the other side of the bayou without being seen. The pirogue had toppled over and had eventually floated to the other side. They were too busy shielding themselves from an array of gunfire, so they missed their ride.

Carsyn was busy trying to devise a plan when she heard footsteps approach. She tugged on the bottom of the blanket and lay still, afraid to even breath. The boat shook as she felt the person step into it and then the sound of the engine lowering into the water. The motor cranked and a low hum vibrated through the air. Carsyn knew a lot of people that lived on the bayou but in the earlier chaos, she didn't pay attention to where she was, and the boat house didn't look familiar.

She stayed hidden for two reasons: She wasn't sure who to trust and she didn't want to put anyone else in danger. At first, she'd thought that maybe they were going to retrieve the pirogue, but they had been riding for several minutes and didn't appear to be slowing down. She prayed that they were going up the bayou toward Crown Point instead of farther down.

The boat stopped and the engine shut off. It rocked from the wake then she felt the person step out. She stayed still afraid that if she moved she would get caught. While she waited she wondered where Levi and Cami were and if they were safe. She knew the answer but chose to hope anyway.

Finally, she lifted the edge of the blanket and peeked out at the empty boat. She stayed on the floor and crawled out from her hiding spot only after she was sure that the dock was empty. She slipped over the side and onto the deck. She recognized the house and for a moment thought about reaching out for help. Deacon's friend Darren lived there and from the floor of the deck she saw that he and their friend Tracy were washing out some ice chests. She realized that it was Tracy's boat that she had been hiding in and wondered how she missed that. She and Deacon had been to his house many times for crab boils and more often to play Pedro with Tracy and his wife Melissa. She couldn't recall ever going into his boat shed so that's probably why it wasn't familiar. She felt relieved because Tracy wasn't a threat but in fact would help her if she asked, both of them would. She felt so conflicted, but her good conscience won the battle.

Carsyn was exhausted and scared and wanted to scream for help, but she couldn't. She wouldn't do that to them. Tears clouded her vision as she made the hard decision to continue on her own. She crawled across the deck of the dock, slipped over the side onto the lawn and watched as they disappeared from her vision. She was only about five miles from her house and the church.

Carsyn froze in place. She let her body go limp onto the ground. She had just realized that she couldn't go home and wasn't sure if she should go back to the church. It hadn't occurred to her before then, but she had nowhere to go. And what scared her even more was that she had no one to help her. She wanted to call out for Cami but was afraid that Levi needed her more than she did at the moment. The tears streamed down her face again and she gave in to a full blown meltdown. She cried it out and then when there were no more tears to shed, she stood up and dried her eyes. *You are strong. You can face any storm. You are the storm. Be the storm.* Carsyn repeated the words over again and eventually started to believe them. She started walking and picked up the pace as she felt she was growing stronger.

Her mind cleared and adrenaline set in as she went over the last conversation she had with Levi. *Detective Stevens! He said I could trust him!* Relief spilled over her like a bucket of cool water on a hot summer day. She wasn't alone after all. She stopped walking again when it registered that she didn't have a phone or anyway to contact him. *God! I feel like I'm losing my mind!* She squeezed her head with both hands and wanted to scream but she refused to go down the pity road again. Besides, there was no one around to care anyway.

She tossed around a few different plans in her head then settled on one. She knew that it was the most dangerous choice and if circumstances weren't favorable she would have to pull out, but it felt like her only hope. She was going home. She hoped that Deacon was still staying at the rental and that she could slip in unnoticed. If she could get another boat, she could pull up in the bayou behind their house and slip in through the back. No one would see her coming.

Again, she was glad she lived in that area because everyone had boats, and most were in the water ready to go. She only had to go down a few more houses to find a small boat that would be perfect for her. *I'm gonna owe a lot of people when this is all over.* The area was quiet, so she jumped into the boat, started the small engine and headed home.

She passed a few people out on the water but most of them were kids joy riding with friends not concerned with her. When she reached the bayou that ran behind her house, she hesitated but knew that was her only way to get to the detective. She'd hashed out a plan while riding down the bayou and decided to dock behind her neighbor's house and walk through the woods to her own backyard. That way, if she were quiet, she'd have a better chance of getting away if anyone were at her home.

The house was dark, and she was relieved to see that Deacon's truck wasn't in the driveway. She stepped onto the back patio and peeked into the huge picture window. Everything was quiet and still, so she exhaled the breath that she had been subconsciously holding. She touched the doorknob and adrenalin shot through her body. She hadn't been home for a while, and it felt natural walking to the back door like the million times she'd done before. That feeling was quickly replaced by anxiety as she turned the knob. *Locked.* She didn't know why she was surprised but she was and found herself unsure what to do next. Then, she ran to the place where they stored the spare key and fished it out from its hiding place.

Relief gave way to encouragement when she inserted the key, turned the knob, and pushed open the door. She stepped into her kitchen and looked around the room with grateful eyes. She didn't turn on the light but instead shut the door behind her and moved away from the window. She was afraid that they were still watching her house and maybe even expected her to return home. She wondered if they knew all along that she would because up until a few hours ago, she didn't think she would come back until the men chasing her were caught and her life was no longer threatened.

She was grateful that she hadn't disconnected her land-line phone because she wanted to get rid of it a while ago, but Deacon refused. He felt that even though they seldom used it, it was necessary in case their cell phone's went down. At the time she'd thought he was overreacting but glad he did. She raced to the phone, reached out to grab the receiver, then hesitated.

She backed up slowly and thought that maybe using the phone right away wasn't the best idea. What if her phone was bugged or the detective's phone? If the people chasing her were as dangerous as Levi says, then they must have people in prominent places on their payroll. She wasn't going to spend a lot of time at her house, but she did want to look around and regroup.

She walked to her bedroom and was saddened by the complete mess they left it in. They had emptied every drawer, pulled them completely out, toppled over every picture and any décor around. They had obviously searched every inch of her room. She would bet that the laundry room was in the same condition because Cami said they were all over her house.

She grabbed a duffle bag that was thrown onto the floor and started to gather a few things she thought she might need. She changed her clothes and considered a quick shower but thought better of it because she needed to be ready to run if anyone showed up. She did go into the bathroom to clean up before heading back to the phone. On her way out of her room she noticed a picture frame broken on the floor. It was a photo of her, Deacon, and Cami at the beach. She fumbled with the frame and broken glass, removed the photo, and shoved it into her pocket.

Carsyn pushed aside the urge to hang around a little longer and headed to the kitchen to call Detective Stevens. She said a quick prayer that he was in the office and would answer the phone. She dialed the number for the local police department and asked for his extension.

"Detective Stevens"

"This is Carsyn. I need your help."

"Carsyn, thank God. Where are you?"

"I don't have a lot of time, but I need your help. Levi said to contact you."

"Is he with you?" Detective Stevens sounded optimistic.

"No, they took him." The phone went silent.

"Do you remember the last time we met? Can you meet me there?"

She hesitated before answering. "Yes. I'll get there but we have to hurry. We have to help Levi. He's in trouble."

"Carsyn, listen to me. I'm on it. Don't worry about Levi, just get to the meeting spot."

Before she could answer, the line went dead.

She hung up the receiver and headed to the door. She stopped to look around her kitchen hoping that she could return soon. She walked out of the house without looking back, now focused on ending this nightmare she'd been living for days. She crossed the yard, jumped into the boa, and headed to their designated meeting place, the Church. Levi said she could trust the Detective and she prayed to God that he was right.

CHAPTER FORTY-SIX

As she drew closer to her destination, her anxiety went up a few levels. Doubt was clouding her judgement, and she was afraid she was making the wrong decision. She wondered how the people chasing after her were able to find her so often. She thought the men in the white van had originally followed her from the Church but once she and Avery lost them, how did they find her again? She had so many unanswered questions. The idea that her only option for help was Detective Stevens didn't sit well with her but for lack of a better idea she agreed.

She docked the small boat and jumped onto the bank. She was growing tired of ending up in these woods and hoped it would all be over soon. *Surely the Detective could protect me. And he must've call in for back up to help save Levi.* She made her way forward but stopped at the edge of the wooded area and looked for his car. The parking lot was empty. Carsyn decided to hold up where she was until he arrived, just in case.

The image of the veil came to her mind directing her focus to that area. *Is it still there?* Her tense body relaxed as sweet memories of seeing Cami again warmed her heart and calmed her soul. She still didn't understand anything about the veil but was grateful that it had existed and allowed her to reconnect with her sister.

The sounds of a car approaching reached her ears and she snapped back to the unsettling reality she was living. She backed up just enough to take cover under the shadows of the trees. She knew she had to be smart and patient and had to make sure it was the Detective before she revealed herself. She'd figured out they were tracking her somehow, but she hoped she had some time before they could get to her position.

She couldn't recall ever seeing the Detective's car, so she waited until the person emerged from the dark sedan that had pulled up next to the church. Carsyn was relieved to see it was Detective Stevens, so she moved closer to the edge of the woods and into the light of the afternoon sky. She caught his attention and waved as she walked slowly toward him. When she was halfway to him, two other cars rolled slowly into the parking lot. *Thank God he called for backup.* She kept walking and eventually stopped next to him. Immediately the hair on her arms stood up and her heart fluttered and almost stopped the moment she looked into his eyes. She was right! She couldn't trust him!

She turned to make a run for the woods, but he grabbed her by her arm and pulled her back.

"Where do you think you're going?" His voice was deep and sinister.

Carsyn tried to break free, but his grip was too tight, and her arm was still sore. She stopped fighting and waited for his next move. The doors of the other cars opened, and large, frightening men dressed in black steeped out. She thought of the skeleton men from the other side of the veil and wondered who scared her the most. She glanced back toward the area where she'd last seen the veil. She needed to get free.

"What are you doing? Let go of me!" Carsyn fell backwards when he released her arm.

"Just give me the chip and we can all go home." The other men had joined Detective Stevens and waited for their instructions.

"I don't know what you're talking about. I don't have anything. And just for the record I knew you were not to be trusted." Tears were stinging her eyes, but she fought to keep them at bay and took a step back away from him.

"Listen to me! I don't care what you know. I just want that chip and I'm tired of playing around. I'm sure Levi told you that some extremely dangerous men are after you, so you know the severity of the situation you're in. Just tell me where the chip is and save yourself a lot of pain."

"I told you! I don't know!" Carsyn took another step back as she screamed at him because she was also tired of playing around and didn't know why they wouldn't listen when she said she didn't have what they wanted.

Another car pulled into the parking lot. Everyone turned their focus to the car, so Carsyn made her move.

She turned to run and this time she was just out of the Detective's reach. She ran as hard as she could toward the veil. Pain shot through her leg, but she pushed through and kept going. The veil appeared just a few feet in front of her. She leaped forward but a hand grabbed her ankle toppling her to the ground. She kicked free and stood up. There were two men attempting to grab her again, but something stopped them. They both froze as they gazed at something above her. She tilted her head upward and saw Cami. The relief she felt spread quickly and then she turned, jumped through the veil, and was gone.

She cowered close to the ground where she had landed waiting to see if they followed her. Her experience so far was that when Cami appeared, everyone went running in the opposite direction. Her body shivered but she wasn't cold. *Deep breaths. Get a grip. You are strong.* Carsyn willed herself to calm down and gain control of her emotions. She wasn't sure but she figured that Levi was in the other car that pulled into the parking lot. She wondered if he realized Detective Stevens had betrayed him. She hoped that he was alright and for a quick moment wondered if he could be trusted. She was glad to see Cami because without her appearance, they would've stopped her from getting away.

While she was still deep in her thoughts, the veil appeared out of thin air, as it usually did, and this time spit out Cami and Levi. She stood up ready to fight before she realized it was the two of them. She rushed over and wanted to leap with joy on top of them but instead waited while they got to their feet.

Carsyn dove into Cami's arms so thankful to see her. Levi's left eye was swollen and bleeding from a cut above his brow, and his cheeks were bruised but overall he looked okay.

"We should move! These men were surprised to see Cami, but it won't take them long to regain their composure and come after us. The men they answer to are much scarier than a ghost" He looked at Cami. "Sorry."

Cami tore away from Carsyn and told Levi that he was probably right. "I'm gonna jump back through and see what's going on."

"No! No! Cami you can't leave me again. Please, let's just move together like Levi said." Carsyn was crying and had a dreadful feeling that she was about to lose Cami again. "Listen. Please. Cami I love you."

"I love you too, but…"

"No! You are not leaving me. Please, I'm scared. Please don't leave."

Cami backed away from Carsyn with tears welling up in her own eyes. She motioned for Levi to step in for her as she continued to watch her baby sister fall apart. "It's the only way. I love you Carsyn. Always remember that I love you."

Carsyn screamed! She tried to shake off Levi's grip and go after Cami, but he held her tight. "Please! Please! Please!" She watched as Cami disappeared. The harder she fought the tighter he held her until she collapsed in his arms.

"I'm sorry." Levi wanted to comfort her but knew there was nothing he could say that would help.

After a momentary breakdown, Carsyn pushed away from Levi and headed for the Veil.

"Whoa, where do you think you're going?" He grabbed her wrist.

"Leave me alone! I have to get to Cami." She charged forward pulling him with her.

"Stop! Please just stop for a minute. I know what they want. You have what they want Carsyn, and you won't be safe as long as you keep it."

Carsyn swung around to face Levi. "I told you I don't have anything for them!"

"Yes you do." Levi released her wrist and held out his hand pleading with her to stop and listen to him. He reached over and touched her shoulder. "It's here. The chip is in your shoulder!"

Carsyn went still.

"When my brother-n-law discovered what the people he was working for were up to, he hid his work in a small chip. He knew that they had altered the technology and that it was dangerous to mankind, so he stole it. He had plans to destroy the chip, but they caught up with him before he got the chance. He knew when he was at Hobby Lobby that they were going to kill him and take the chip, so he injected it into your arm." He waited for her to catch up before he went on. "The chip is in your arm. I'm not entirely sure what the technology can do but he did say that it was somewhat like virtual reality and could control people's minds. He referred to the technology as "AI" and warned of its danger. Do you know anything about Artificial Intelligence? The last thing he said to me was that it would be extremely dangerous if it got into the wrong hands."

Carsyn touched her shoulder and felt the familiar bump. Everything Levi was saying sounded bizarre, but it made sense to her now. She recalled the slight sting she felt when the man bumped into her, but the force of the impact was so strong that she forgot about the sting. And she was stunned by the whole thing and at the same time preoccupied with being followed. She was still speechless as she revisited the whole ordeal.

"Carsyn." Levi tried to get her attention. He hated hurrying her, but they were running out of time. He grabbed her shoulders. "Carsyn, I know this is a lot but we gotta get it out of your arm now. Cami won't be able to stop those men for long."

Carsyn looked into his eyes and saw compassion. She shuddered as his words registered. She knew what he was saying was necessary, but that didn't make it any less terrifying. She wished Cami were there. She was terrified and needed support. She reached into her pocket and took out the photo of herself, Deacon, and Cami and held onto it for comfort.

She watched as Levi pulled something from his pocket. Her body went limp, and she collapsed to the ground.

Her world was spinning out of control again because just before she slipped into the darkness, she noticed the Cross that was engraved into the pocketknife he was holding over her. The impact of his betrayal sucked the air out of her lungs, and her eyes went vacant.

CHAPTER FORTY-SEVEN

Carsyn heard voices before she opened her eyes. The room was dark, so she was having trouble locating where the sound was coming from. The light from the small television mounted on the wall flickered and grabbed her attention. Panic surged through her when she realized that she was back in the hospital. She wanted to scream but instead talked herself into staying calm. She remembered that every time this happened she eventually transported back to where she was.

The vision of Levi holding the pocketknife was almost unbearable as it slammed into her mind and caused her to gasp. She managed to compose herself and patiently laid there waiting to get back. Deacon was sleeping in the chair next to her bed and although she wanted badly to jump into his lap and let him wrap his arms around her, and protect her, she knew that it wasn't safe. Not yet. She closed her eyes and waited. She squeezed them tighter as time passed. *Something's wrong. Why am I still here?* She began to worry but wasn't giving up yet. She had to get back there and finish things.

She stayed completely still and waited, trying to be patient, and eventually fell asleep. When she woke up in the hospital again, she bolted out of the bed and called out for Cami. She stood up and tried to run to the door but the pain in her leg was back just as fierce as when she was first shot.

Her screams for Cami woke Deacon and he ran to her side. He tried to comfort her, but she was out of control and beyond comforting.

"Cami! Cami! Where are you? Cami!" She leaned against the bed and frantically looked around the room waiting for her sister to appear. She pushed Deacon away and continued to call out for Cami.

Deacon buzzed for the nurse while he tried to calm his wife down.

She continued to scream and plead and call out for Cami and Levi. She didn't know what was happening. "Where are you Cami? I need you!"

Two nurses ran into the room and tried to help Deacon subdue her. They finally got her back into the bed and gave her a shot to calm her down. The effects of the shot were slow as she continued to call out. Finally, Carsyn's screams for her sister were nothing more than a whisper and her body began to relax.

"Carsyn, honey, it's okay. Do you know where you are?" Deacon was a wreck but tried to comfort his wife.

"Why am I still here? Where is Cami? Where is Levi?" Her eyes pleaded for answers that he didn't have.

"You were shot Carsyn. They brought you to the hospital a few days ago with a gunshot wound to your leg. Don't you remember?"

She began to feel agitated again, but the medicine continued to work and kept her calm. She closed her eyes and willed herself back to Cami. She listened to Deacon as he continued to explain what had happened to her.

"Carsyn, you were carjacked. A few days ago you were carjacked and shot in the leg. Someone found you..."

Her eyes sprung open. "What did you say?"

"You were carjacked."

"No. You said a few days ago. That's not right. It's been longer than that. I was released from the hospital almost two weeks ago. We went home but they found us! We ran to the shop, and they found us there! Deacon, we have to go before they find us again!" She began to sob uncontrollably.

Deacon stroked her hair. "No Carsyn. We never left the hospital."

She tried to get up, but the medicine made her dizzy and disoriented. The tears streamed down the side of her face. She looked at her husband and pleaded with him to listen to her, but he just continued to stroke her hair and reason with her.

"We never left the hospital. You came in with a gunshot wound to the leg. Earlier today, they realized that something was in your injured shoulder, so they took you down for an Xray. Do you remember any of that?"

Carsyn grabbed at her shoulder and found that it was bandaged up. She fought against the effects of the medicine and tried to make Deacon listen to her.

"Deacon you have to listen to me. They are coming for us. We have to get out of here. They want the AI and will stop at nothing to get it back. Where is it? What did they do with the chip that was in my arm?"

Deacon listened to his wife ramble on before he continued. "That's right Carsyn. When they X-rayed your arm they found a small chip, so they had it removed. They didn't know exactly what it was but felt like it was the cause of your recent delusional outbursts."

"No! Yes! It's a chip that contains AI technology and if it gets into the wrong hands it can be dangerous. We have to find Levi and Cami before it's too late."

"You were dreaming Honey. Cami died almost two years ago; don't you remember. You were dreaming. It's not real. Cami's not here sweetheart. She's gone."

His words whirled around and around in her head, but she couldn't accept them. She refused to accept them. He was wrong. Cami was here. She saved her life. "You're wrong Deacon. Cami was here. She saved my life! She saved my life!" Carsyn repeated the words until she succumbed to the sedatives.

A few hours later, the nurse came in to check on her and to change her bandages. When she touched her side, Carsyn woke. She immediately asked for Cami and grew agitated when Deacon repeated that Cami wasn't there and that she was just dreaming. She ignored him and continued to call out for her sister. "CAMI! CAMI! It was not all a dream! She was here! She saved my life! Deacon, she was here. I can't lose her again." She cried because he didn't believe her, and part of her was afraid what he was saying was true. She fought off that idea for a while but when Cami didn't show up she started to mourn for her sister all over again. The more she thought about it the more she continued to cry.

The nurse finished changing the bandages on her leg and arm and helped Carsyn get comfortable in the bed. She lifted the side of Carsyn's gown and commented on how nasty her injury looked and that she must have fallen on something really hard to cause that kind of bruising.

Carsyn abruptly stopped crying, touched her side and simply smiled with joy "Cami." She finally gave into the calming sedative, dropped her arm over the side of the bed and released the photo she had been holding in her hand.

END

ACKNOWLEDGEMENTS

Thanks to my Beta Readers, Pam Volek, Peggy Morgan, Sr. Clared, and Glenn Griffin for their invaluable encouragement and criticism of me and my work.

Thanks to my family and friends for listening to me talk about ideas for my books, day in and day out.

Thanks to my mother for not only sharing her wisdom but also her love of music. Que Sera Sera was one of her favorite songs and when I hear it, I'm filled with precious memories.

Thanks to my husband Glenn Griffin for everything! Your love and support surrounds me every day encouraging me to push forward and reach for my dreams.

Finally, I thank God for all that I am and all that I have. He is always with me, and I give him all Glory! I am a firm believer in signs, and I am thankful for the Grace to be able to recognize them as they come into my life.

Also by
D. M. BOURGEOIS

SLIPPING INTO DARKNESS

MISGUIDED REVENGE

ABOUT THE AUTHOR

D. M. Bourgeois was born in New Orleans and now resides in Crown Point, Louisiana with her husband Glenn. She studied Creative writing at Nicholls State University in Thibodaux, Louisiana. She believes that her life is blessed, and aside from being a mother and grandmother, becoming an author is one of her greatest joys. Her first two novels, SLIPPING INTO DARKNESS, and MISGUIDED REVENGE, were Sliver Falchion Award Finalists in the Best Supernatural category at Killer Nashville Writers Conference.

For more information you can visit D. M. Bourgeois @
Website: dmbourgeois.com
Email: dmbourgeois61@gmail.com
Facebook: dmbourgeois61